I0739156

THE IRISH WARRIOR

ASHLEY YORK

ISBN (print): 0990864065
ISBN-13 (print): 978-0-9908640-6-6
ISBN (ebook): 0990864073
ISBN-13 (ebook): 978-0-9908640-7-3

Cover design: Wicked Smart Designs
Editing: Scott Moreland

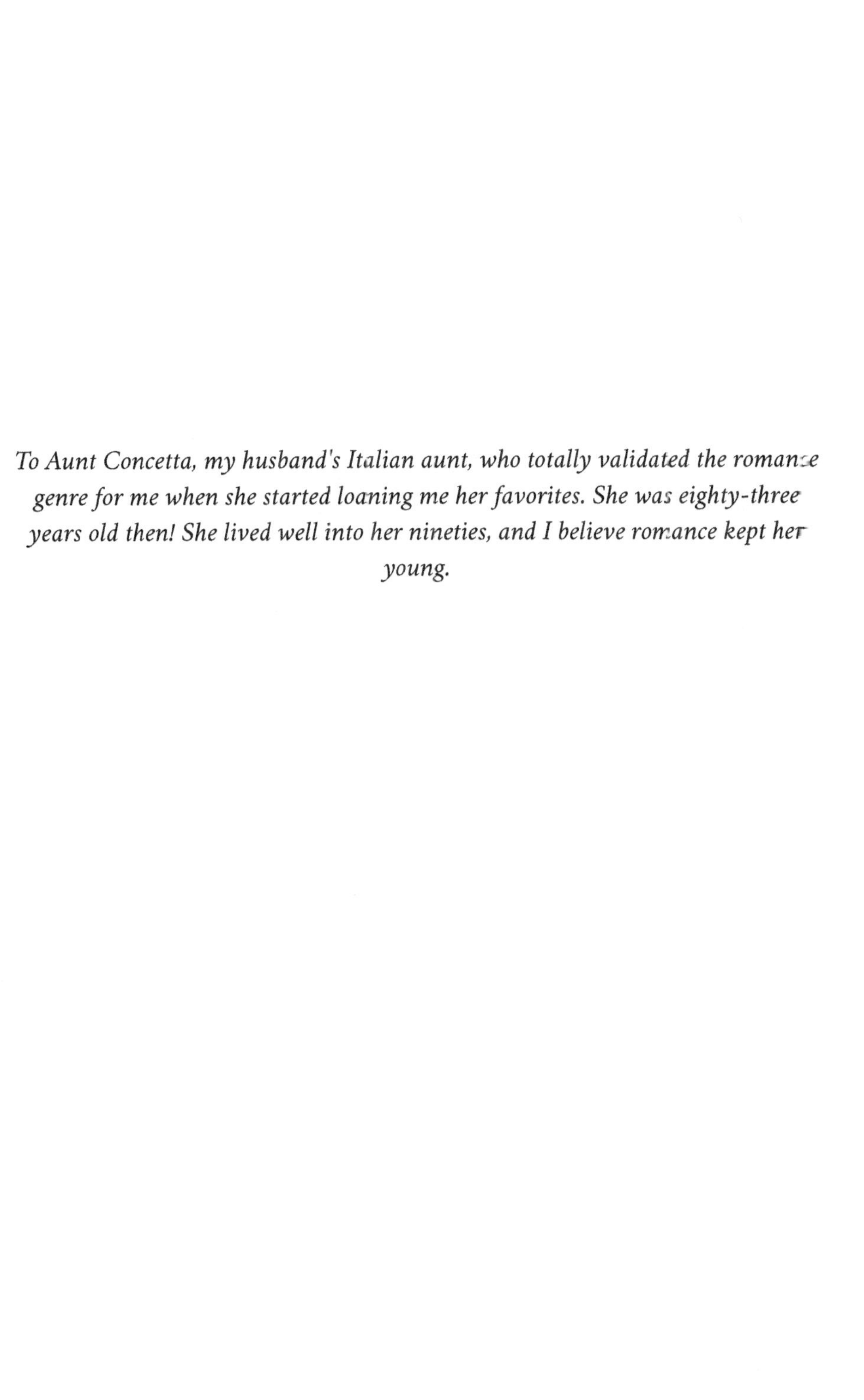

To Aunt Concetta, my husband's Italian aunt, who totally validated the romance genre for me when she started loaning me her favorites. She was eighty-three years old then! She lived well into her nineties, and I believe romance kept her young.

CHAPTER 1

Black Poole, England 1075

Sean of Drogheda was mad enough to spit. Anger squeezed his gut, snaking around any clear thinking he might have managed and choked it until it was good and dead. His fisted hand clenched against his thigh. He urged the horse forward.

His mount reared slightly, pitching its head left then right, nearly unseating Sean. The round, wooden shield secured to his back shook with the movement. Like an arrow, understanding shot through Sean's rage induced state. He immediately loosened the rein from his iron grip and righted the deer hide brat draped over his shoulders. The beast need not suffer from his ill temper.

"Easy, Roana." Sean spoke through gritted teeth. The courser jerked its head in response. "Easy, lass."

Calum Rua pulled up short in front of him and turned his horse about. His sparse red beard did little to hide his scowl of anger and irritation. "Sean! Ye're being an arse."

Sean exhaled slowly, methodically. Heat surged through him. He narrowed his eyes at the man blocking his path. Beating his friend into the ground would be a fine way to release this fury burgeoning inside of him.

Calum's mouth tightened and his nostrils flared as if sensing the unspoken threat. "Damn it. Let. It. Go. 'Tis done. She's wed." He rolled his eyes and tugged the animal to face front and continue forward. "I'll not be yer lackey to be kicked around nor pick ye up when yer mount drops ye on yer arse. I'm for the boat."

Sean watched his friend's retreating back as he galloped away. The tension didn't lessen. The anger didn't lessen. The feeling that his life had been ripped away from him didn't lessen.

Closing his eyes, Sean could again see Brighit's laughing face, her cheeks lightly reddened from the exertion of running up the hill. Nigh on four years ago now but the memory still burned.

He'd let her get ahead of him and believe she was beating him. All so he could watch her fine backside displayed in her brother Tadhg's tight trews and too short leine as she raced ahead. Tadhg would have taken a strap to her if he'd realized she'd dressed that way. Sean selfishly encouraged her rebellion. He'd been stiff as a board when he finally reached her and they collapsed on the hill, side by side, laughing and breathing heavily.

The intensity of emotions flooded back. He'd needed to touch her. Needed it more than his next breath. Anywhere. Caressing. Squeezing. Kissing—that had been what prompted the slap. He'd worked his way closer, covering her with an arm. They'd both grown quiet. And that wide-eyed expression of surprise when his face hovered above hers.

"What are ye about, Sean?" Her eyebrows slashed down, her tone accusing. "Don't ye even—"

But he was way past "even" and her lips were tender and supple. He thought he'd died and gone to heaven. An innocent kiss.

The club to his ear made him cry out in pain.

"What to hell?" Sean said, gripping the side of his head with two hands.

Brighit pushed him away from her and stood, towering over him as he lay at her feet. "Sean! How dare ye take liberties with me! I'm like yer sister."

He cringed inside. Why did she always insist they were like brother and sister? Sean certainly didn't feel that way. He wanted to marry her but she shunned all his advances.

Her hands on her hips, she narrowed her eyes. "I won't tell Tadhg what ye've done here so that ye may continue to live."

She was right. His best friend would kick his arse from here to the Hill if he found out what just happened. He stood, slowly. She took a step back, keeping her distance. Like a fist to the gut, she acted afeared of him. Regret surged through him, dashing any lust-filled thoughts. He did not want her to fear him.

"Please, Brig, I dinna mean to—"

"Yea! Yea, ye did and ye ken it. As do I… now. This is done. I'm not for ye as I've told ye time and time again. Do not be coming around with yer pleas of friendship. I see yer heart clearly now and I'll have none of it."

He started toward her but she held up her hand to ward him off. "Nee! I mean what I say. Ye sit. Sit!"

Unmoving, she waited until he had again settled on the ground.

"I will return alone. Ye may not accompany me."

"Shite! Tad will have my head if I let ye wander through the woods alone."

"YE are what threatens me. YE!" She pointed her finger at him, her eyes bulging with accusation. "I will be safer alone than with ye."

And with that she left him.

Sean sighed and opened his eyes.

And now the love of his life married to some Norman knight? Sean would never have his way with her. What to hell was he supposed to do when every waking thought, and many arousing dreams, had been spent lusting after her? If he were being honest with himself, he'd admit it was her fine body he sought to master. He never imagined her making his food or tending his children, just being betwixt her legs.

Her father and six brothers had kept her well protected but Sean had glimpsed her fiery courage. Her rebellious spirit. Intentionally going against the rules. She longed to let go. She wanted to be free. Now her fine Norman would be unlocking the passion that lay beneath her trained obedience.

Sean kicked his mount into a gallop and slackened the reins. A local animal he'd rented. It knew the area well which he did not. Yet another reason for his gut-wrenching frustration but his anger merely wasted his energy. It truly was over. No chance remained for him. He'd been focused on winning Brighit over for nigh on five years now, believing he would eventually succeed. He showed himself an idiot for being so persistent and not realizing her stubbornness. He had to return to Eire and make a life for himself that didn't include Brighit MacNaughton.

At the top of the rise, he paused to catch his breath. The animal did the same, twitching its ears in exhilaration as if sensing its nearness to home.

"Settle yerself, Roana. We've quite a ways to go yet."

Sean looked out over the wide expanse of water barely visible between the thick forest separating him from his homeland, the cold air filling his lungs. A deep sadness welled up inside. He had to let it go. The anger and resentment did him no good. His dream of wedding the lovely Brighit was like mist on the water. Here then gone.

Sean jumped from his horse. He secured his shield to the saddle. Removing his brat, he folded it up and tucked it underneath. The walk would do him good, give him a chance to get his emotions to settle. With Tadhg staying behind with Brighit, Sean would be acting clan leader once he arrived in Drogheda. He needed to show a calm, thoughtful demeanor. His anger could be his undoing since they all knew how hot-headed he could be. They would watch for him to lose control. Calum's support would be crucial. He shouldn't have let him go on ahead.

A high-pitched whistle sounded from the woods beside him. The courser broke loose from the light hold he'd had of the reins and raced off toward the trees.

"Hey! Stop!" Sean froze in disbelief then began to chase after the animal. "Stop, ye stupid shite."

Finally out of breath and admitting the waste of time chasing a galloping horse was, he went down to one knee. A few feet from the forest's edge, he'd swear he heard a female laugh. He steadied his breathing so he could listen. Yes, definitely someone laughing. He stood, peering into the darkness of the trees, hands fisted on his hips. The sun rested low in the sky and cast little light within.

He ground his teeth in irritation. Someone had called to the animal, truly enjoying a laugh at his expense. A coward, hiding in the dark. The low jingle of the iron stirrups indicated the horse and rider were not far, just beyond his sight.

Sean took a few steps into the woods, allowing his eyes to adjust. The shadowed figure of the mounted animal became discernible. It whinnied and backed further into the darkness.

"Hold!" Sean said. He struggled not to let his anger be heard. "Ye've bested me. Steal the horse but I'm for the coast. I need my things."

"'Tis not stealing it if it's mine."

Not a woman's voice. A young lad then.

"I paid for the use of it, son."

"I'm not yer son." The voice broke, confirming Sean's suspicions.

"Nae. Ye're not but I have quite a walk ahead of me. May I at least collect my belongings?"

A loud thud accompanied the bag that dropped at his feet. Sean stared at the sack. Arrogant little shite. The few items he'd collected to bring home were no doubt in pieces now. Anger simmered. He glanced toward the rider.

"My thanks. And will ye toss the weapons at me as well?"

"They're mine now… the price for the use of my horse."

Sean forced himself to appear calm. "I told ye I paid for the use."

"But it wasn't paid to me."

Sean moved in closer but with every step, the rider retreated. If he could get his hands on him, Sean would teach him a lesson he wouldn't soon be forgetting. By his size, the boy looked to be about ten.

"But I did pay for its use. An honest agreement between men. I had nae way of knowing it had been stolen. I had plans to return it." Despite the blood racing through him at being outsmarted by some unknown, he shifted his tactics. He used his ever-so-amicable tone of voice but would not be letting the horse—or rider—get away. "When was the horse stolen from ye?"

The lad didn't respond at first but the beast shifted, indicating uneasiness. "It was taken without my permission."

Sean gave a small smile, moving closer as he spoke. "That's what I said."

"Nae ye asked when it was stolen from me."

"Is there a difference?"

The lad tipped his head back as if looking heavenward in exasperation. Taking his eyes off Sean proved to be his mistake. With three long strides Sean closed in, yanked at the reins, and ripped them from the rider's loose grip. Stepping clear, he waited while the courser jerked against the rope now held firmly in his grip. The rider, struggling to keep his seat, tossed about with the rough motion.

"*Arghhh.*"

Definitely a young lad. Not even a curse uttered from the unexpected change of events.

"Damn it."

Sean smiled and stepped in to put his arm around the horse's snout to settle it down. He spoke in a quiet, calming voice. "Easy now, Roana."

"Roana! What kind of name is that?" The lad threw his leg over the far side of its body in preparation for his escape.

The courser was not very tall. Sean wondered why he didn't just jump off.

"The one I gave it! A handsome beast deserves a handsome name."

He grabbed at the lad's skinny arm, hauling him across the saddle, flat on his belly, facing him.

Sean offered a contented smile. "Did ye have somewhere to go?"

The horse thief kicked his legs and strained against Sean's unwavering grip.

"Let me loose!" He all but screeched in his outrage.

"I dunna take kindly to someone stealing my mount."

"I told ye. 'Tis *my* mount." He yanked and pulled.

Sean took hold of his little shoulders and dragged him forward, dropping him hard on the ground beside him. The horse skittered away but didn't seem inclined to stray very far despite the commotion. Sean held the end of the reins fast.

When the boy tried to stand, Sean shoved him back down with the toe of his boot. The thief landed on his backside with a loud *oomph.*

"Sit!" Sean stroked the horse with a soothing *shhh* between orders. "Stay!"

The boy sat with his knees pulled up tight to his body, shooting daggers at Sean. He had a young face from what Sean could see. A pretty face for a boy with reddish-brown hair pulled back.

"Were ye lying in wait for yer horse? If it even is yer horse."

"'Tis my horse!" The boy lurched forward, his cheeks a bright red, and he spat the words at Sean then slammed his lips together and crossed his arms. The bright, green eyes held the telltale glistening of tears. Tears?

"Buck up, man." Sean understood the lad's frustration but to have him crumbling would be thoroughly embarrassing. "A slower man than I would have had quite a walk ahead and nae way to defend himself against brigands he may find along the way. And that after he had paid honestly for the use of the horse."

"She was not theirs to lend out." The lad jutted out his chin. "'Tis my horse and I've been searching for it. And ye're not so fast."

"Fast enough."

The lad swiped at the tear dripping off his chin then looked away. "Go ahead. Take her. See if I care."

Sean moved in close to the animal and removed his long sword from the scabbard with a slow, fluid movement. The boy stood, alert now, watching him. His eyes widened with fear.

"Ye want me to take her? Now?" Sean turned toward him and held the formidable weapon upright as if inclined to use it. "Take her? As in I would then be stealing *yer* horse?"

The boy took a step back. And then another. Finally backing against the trunk of a large oak tree.

"Ye *would* be stealing it," he said, his voice quiet.

The horse seemed alert to the lad as if she did belong to the boy. Sean was inclined to believe his story. Why lie? Truth to tell he only needed it as far as the sea. Once he had the knife back that he'd offered up as collateral, he didn't care who took the animal. The rounded shoulders of the lad, the stench of living in the rough, and the way he kept glancing toward the animal made Sean feel a bit sorry for him. Mayhap an agreement could be reached.

"So ye say the horse was stolen from ye?"

"Taken without permission," the boy corrected.

Was he being intentionally obstinate? "I dunna see the difference."

"Of course ye dunna."

Sean tipped his head toward the boy, his brows raised. Blood pumped in his ears at the innuendo. "*Of course* I dunna?"

"Ye're too stupid to understand the distinction."

Distinction? Sean's mouth opened slightly at such audacity from one so young. "What did ye call me?"

The boy stood a little taller, barely coming up as far as Sean's chest. "Ye heard me."

Sean took a step closer and glanced at his sword before him. "I dunna believe I did."

"Ye're an islander. Ye're stupid." The boy's hands reached around the trunk of the tree.

It seemed as though the boy was just leaning against it, but then Sean saw the club he'd reached for.

Sean grabbed him by the tunic, yanking him off the ground, pulling him in close to his face. Their noses nearly touching. The large club that had been hidden behind the tree dropped harmlessly from his grasp.

"Were ye going to brain me with that?"

The lad took a shaky breath. His entire body trembled while his feet dangled beneath him.

"So yer bravery came from yer weapon?" Sean looked him over, grimacing, to convey his disgust at what he saw. "Not much of a man are ye?"

The nostrils flared. "And ye threatened me with yer sword. What does that say about ye?"

Point well taken. Still fisting his tunic, Sean allowed his feet to touch the ground now. Long lashes framed almond-shaped eyes that held his own. To say this lad was pretty would be an understatement. *If* he was a girl, he'd be—she'd be quite comely. He glanced at his hand that lay nearly flush against the heaving chest. Clearly if it was a girl, she was trying to hide the fact. Despite what the lad might think about Sean's intelligence, he was clever enough to figure out someone's sex.

"Let me go." The lad's bravery had returned and he tried to break free. "Take my horse and leave me."

And now he was giving orders.

"Take yer horse?" Sean searched his face. The tracks left clean from the tears gave him pause. "So ye can whistle it out from under me? Or so ye can say I stole it from ye and have me whipped? But then again, ye've given me yer permission. Or is there nae longer a *distinction*?"

The scowl said the lad was mad enough to spit. "I willna bother ye one way or the other."

"So says the thief."

"I'm nae thief."

"Ye stole my horse from me!" Sean said.

"'Tis my horse!" The pitch of his voice rose a bit.

Sean glanced around the darkened woods. He saw no sign of anyone else. No trails leading away. No place that could be used for shelter. If this were a lass, she had no business being here. Mayhap that was reason enough to dress as a boy.

"Is no one with ye?"

His eyes widened ever so slightly, revealing flecks of gold even in the waning light. "Why?"

Defensive. It wasn't looking good. Sean indicated the club on the ground beside her. "Yer only protection?"

"I can protect myself just fine. Unhand me." She pulled at his hand. "Isn't that why ye willna drop yer weapon? Because I *can* defend myself?"

Sean smirked. He shoved her away with a well-placed push to her chest which was far more fleshy than it should have been. She adjusted her shirt with narrowed eyes, searching his face as if to assess if he'd uncovered the truth. He had, but she didn't need to know. He kept his features blank. Sean placed his weapon on the ground, carefully, crossed his arms and stared her down.

She shrugged. "So? Leave! Go! Take her."

"I am waiting for answers but my patience wears thin. Do I need to take ye over my knee?"

Her hands moved instinctively to cover her backside. Well, someone had disciplined the lass despite her mouthiness.

She averted his gaze. "I am not alone. I am here with my brother. We search for my horse," she turned a stern look on him, "which I have now found."

She lied through her teeth. But a brother? The now obvious filling out of her tunic indicated she was probably of a marriageable age so why not a husband?

"Ye're with yer brother? I see nae sign of a brother. Just a lad alone in the woods, getting himself into trouble."

Her cheeks blazed with color. "He went to see if he could track down my horse."

Her irritated tone bordered on insulting.

"And he told ye to stay put?"

She was also probably told to stay hidden.

"He's returning any moment." Her cheeks darkened.

He tried not to smile at her transparency. "Methinks not." A bad liar. "Might I ken yer name?"

Her full brows dipped into a V. "Why?"

"So that when we travel together on yer horse, I'll ken what to call ye."

Her jaw dropped.

"Nae? Ye'd rather I take yer horse and leave ye here? Rather than take ye to this brother with the very horse he is supposedly searching for?"

He'd swear he could hear her jumbled thoughts as she tried to work out her answer. She was a very bad liar.

"A name is all I'm asking." He fought the urge to roll his eyes. Instead he used his most acquiescent tone. "I promise not to use it against ye."

Her lips puckered. "Thomas—Tommy. Call me Tommy."

For some reason her expression no longer indicated she lied. "Now we make progress, *Tommy*. And ye may call me Sean. Apologize for yer insults and I'll see ye safely to yer brother."

She gasped. "Nae! I'll not apologize. I only stated the truth."

"The truth? Dear *Tommy*, I fear if the truth were a snake, ye'd get bitten in the arse."

"How dare ye!"

Hmm, perhaps she was not worried about being revealed as a female—not as much as she should be. A reminder may be in order. "*How dare I? What are ye? A girl?*"

"Nae!" Her protest sounded a little too strong. She seemed to sense it and snapped her mouth shut.

The last thing Sean needed was to travel to town with her but he needed the horse. He also didn't need it known that his traveling companion was a female only pretending to be a boy. Villages along the coast were full of unscrupulous travelers—all male—who wouldn't mind finding a female in their midst. He didn't need to be put in the position of having to protect her.

"Good! Because I've nae need to be seen with a female dressed in lad's clothing. There are plenty of men looking for just that sort of sport, I assure ye, but I am not."

Sean didn't miss her gaping mouth but returned his sword, secured his items and turned the horse about. He leapt into the saddle and reached his arm down to *Tommy.* If he had to travel to town with her, he'd just as soon she continue with her disguise. The idea of catering to a whining female right now did not sit well with him. He needed to get back home and put this whole terrible trip behind him. The sooner the better.

CHAPTER 2

homasina glanced at the large hand being offered her.

"Again I wait." Sean said. "Give me yer arm."

She had no idea how to jump onto a horse but every young boy did. She'd better learn quickly. Just as she began to lift her hand up, the huge, bearded man leaned forward to grab it and yanked her up behind him.

Pain shot through her shoulder and she leaned forward in agony.

"Reidh?"

Ready? Thomasina cringed, holding her breath to keep the groan of pain from escaping. She took a deep swallow. "Aye. Reidh."

As one, they lurched forward with the movement. Her beloved beast moved beneath them. Her own pain forgotten as she felt for any shift of a misplaced hoof or strained ligament, any sign her horse had been mistreated while separated from her. This man certainly did not seem like someone who would be cruel to an animal.

A big man, yea. Towered over her. But he didn't seem mean. Even his back was expansive. She couldn't see anything beyond it. His body narrowed at the waist so that her legs were only somewhat indecently surrounding him, resting against his own thighs. She needed to lose him.

No doubt this man meant to help her search for her brother but he wouldn't be found. Damn him. Why couldn't Niall be where she needed

12

him to be? He'd never have left her behind to deal with her father alone. She thought she'd only have to wait a few days but she'd waited nigh a week. Alone in that dark cave with only the food she could catch or gather to eat.

"Sean?" Thomasina coughed and adjusted her voice to a lower pitch and hoped the man hadn't heard the slip. "Sean?"

What sounded like a chuckle preceded his answer. "Aye?"

"Can ye tell me who had my horse?"

A massive lift of his broad shoulders his only reply. He pushed the horse into a trot once they cleared the trees.

It had been bad enough that her father willingly handed her off to the highest bidder but separating her from her horse as well had been too much.

"If I knew the name, it might help me... stop the person from taking her again."

A loud sigh followed. Sean slowed the horse until they stopped.

"I can't hear ye, *Tommy.*"

Something about the way he said her name, made her think she irritated him.

"I'm sorry, Sean." She liked saying his name, the way it sounded to her ears. He had a strange accent as well but she dare not question him. He'd already shown his short temper and she didn't require another display. "I would appreciate ye taking me back and showing me where ye first saw my horse."

"Is that it?" Sean turned toward her but did not look directly at her.

"I dunna ken what yer asking."

"Is that all ye had to tell me?"

His irritation came from her asking a question? He didn't want her to talk!

"Aye." She clamped her mouth shut and crossed her arms in front of her. Insolent man.

The sun quickly dropping, Thomasina didn't know the area. She also didn't know how far it was to where he had gotten her horse. He spurred the animal again, faster this time.

"Hold tight, lad." Sean ordered with a loud voice.

She didn't know what he meant but held the horse tighter with her legs.

"Hold, lad." He shouted the words at her. "Just do it."

"I ken not—"

"Damn." Sean muttered and grabbed her right hand, wrapping it around his firm torso. The movement shifted Thomasina forward in the saddle, all but flattening her against his back.

Damn is right. She tried to pull back slightly to stop her breasts from crushing against him. He wouldn't be expecting her to have any breasts and as far as breasts go, hers weren't very big, so maybe he wouldn't notice.

"The other hand, too!" he said in a growl but gave the horse its lead to let loose before she could wrap the other arm about him.

Sean seemed to care very little for her struggles or discomfort. When she had him encircled in her arms, he covered both her hands with his own much larger one as if to keep them there. His warm palm was calloused. His fingers strong where they gripped her wrist. He urged the horse into a fast gallop as if the devil himself were chasing them.

She tried not to breathe too deep to stop anything from moving against him. It hadn't even occurred to her to bind her breasts when she'd gone off after her brother. She'd been desperate to get away from her father bellowing after her when she'd run to get her horse. Dressing like a boy should have been enough. All she needed to do was to go find Niall and get his help escaping her father's demands until he sobered. Surely then he'd realize the horrible mistake he'd made in offering her as payment to clear his debts.

Sean's legs relaxed against hers. The horse responded immediately and they were trotting then walking when they again entered the woods. Behind her, a sudden downpour started. They were mostly protected by the thick trees.

Sean released her hands before jumping off the horse. Thomasina paused but a moment before rolling onto her belly and sliding down the horse. She could feel his eyes on her but when she turned to look, he was walking away from her to the edge of the clearing.

He shook his head, clearly irritated. He looked out through the pouring rain. The rain so loud, he had to shout. "Doubt it will let up until morning."

That must have been why he'd started racing. He knew of the impending storm. It was miserable. The rain made everything cold and damp. Thomasina hugged herself for warmth. Whatever angered him— and the deep scowl on his face did indeed indicate his anger—had nothing to do with her. All she did was try to get her horse back.

Thomasina went to her horse, seeking the comfort of a friend. She rubbed her hands down the length of her appreciative beast. "Ye're looking well cared for."

"Of course she's well cared for." She hadn't heard him coming toward her. "Do ye think I beat my animals?"

Thomasina stepped back as the man removed the items from its back.

"I dunna think anything. I have sorely missed her. I am glad she is unharmed."

Sean rested an arm on the horse's bare back, facing her with a smirk. "And if not for ye, the horse could not possibly survive?"

Without waiting for her reply, he pushed off. He paused and looked about the area before setting the items on the ground. "Either we can be warm with the skins atop or be protected from the cold ground with it on the bottom. I say the top." He shook out the large length of deer skin as he spoke then stopped to pierce her with his bright, blue eyes. "What say ye?"

He had deep set eyes that sparkled even in the forest's dimness.

"Um, yea, 'tis fine."

She wasn't certain why she kept feeling like she needed to defend herself. Perhaps because he seemed so damned angry. "What would ye have me do?"

Sean looked her up and down then smiled. The type of smile that wasn't real. An attempt to hold in his annoyance no doubt. "Nothing. Ye'd best stay here. I will see to the food."

Thomasina wanted to come to the defense of the boy he believed her to be. Why would he act like she couldn't do anything? Look at all she'd accomplished. She'd gotten her horse back. She'd defended herself against someone much bigger and stronger, despite the tremors that had washed over her at the sight of him. Who could blame her? He was huge, like a mountain, towering in front of her with large, muscular arms that could squeeze the life out of her no doubt. The arms of a warrior. She had held her ground and done pretty well for a boy. Even better for a woman.

Thomasina moved about gathering wood for a fire. A nice blaze awaited Sean when he returned a short while later. He glanced her way a few times but said nothing as he prepared what he'd caught. She turned away from the disgusting sight of having the—whatever—skinned and cooked. Her stomach growled at the aroma of the meat sizzling over the flames.

They ate in silence. The rain kept up with occasional fat drops that worked their way through the thick canopy to plop on them. It wasn't long before she was being bitten by a variety of irritating bugs.

"Oh, damn." Thomasina slapped the bug on her arm. Blood oozed across her soaked sleeve.

Sean sat leaning against a fallen log, oblivious, staring into the flames. His long, powerfully built legs stretched out in front of him. He'd retrieved a skin from his sack which he drank from at steady intervals without offering to share. They'd already found a nearby brook with water for drinking so she assumed it must be something stronger.

"Devil spawn." She slapped another bug dead.

Sean turned his bright eyes on her, his brows low as if thinking through a problem. His long hair hung behind him, pulled back at the crown. Not really blond. More the color of wheat but it looked soft to the touch. He seemed to see right through her.

"Shite!" She slapped at her leg. She must be one tasty morsel according to all these bugs and he sat there totally unbothered.

At least in the cave there had been no flying things to feast on her, just a few bats that kept to their own area. It had also seemed much safer than this place, less exposed. She glanced into the darkness. She couldn't make out anything beyond the light from the fire.

"Whoreson!" She slapped at her neck and her hand came back bloody. "What to hell!"

Sean raised his eyebrows now clearly contemplating her. As if she spoke a language he didn't understand. As if he were just noticing her at all.

"Ye have quite a mouth on ye." He sounded as if he were making an observation. No expression. "Let me ken when ye run out of expletives. I'll be happy to supply yer youthful brain with words nae child should ken."

"I'm not a child."

Sean swept his gaze over her body and she felt the sudden urge to shield herself from his view. When he looked her in the face, he smiled. A knowing smile. A smile that said "I know yer secret".

"I would not say ye're a man yet. Would ye, *Tommy*?"

Thomasina seethed inside at her own prideful outburst.

Idiot!

Of course she was a child. Just a boy. Not a lass of ten and eight only pretending to be a boy.

Sean kept his eyes on her face. He watched but said nothing. The shadows cast from the fire played across the strong planes of his face. She shivered.

"Are ye cold, *Tommy*?" His voice pitched lower this time. He took a long drink, his eyes never leaving her.

She wrapped her arms across her chest, hugging herself. "Nae."

He licked his lips as if whatever he drank were delicious.

A fluttering inside demanded… action. She held out her hand to him. "May I have some?"

"'Tis best not to indulge at such a young age." His tone remained even but that light in his eyes intensified as if he were holding back laughter.

She kept her hand out. "Please," she coughed again. "Please."

Satisfied that her voice sounded more appropriate, she tipped her nose into the air. She tried for that I-will-not-back-down expression that boys get.

His white teeth gleamed and he took another swallow. "Are ye certain?"

Her hand did not waver and it suddenly seemed of the utmost importance that she taste whatever he was drinking. She was not much of a drinker. Her father imbibed too often and too much. She preferred not to be like him. This seemed different somehow. The need to win this stranger's acquiescence pushed her.

"Yea."

His eyes pierced hers. She felt the jolt down to her toes and she couldn't explain it. As he moved forward to pass her the skin, his eyes never wavered. They held hers as if in a trance. His warm fingers brushed her palm. Lightning shot up her arm.

"Thank ye." Her voice sounded breathy.

She glanced at the glistening, pink lips just visible through his heavy beard. His eyes remained on hers. She took a sip. Bitter liquid burned down her throat and she jumped to her feet. Grimacing, she spit it onto the ground.

"Now that is a waste," he said.

"What to hell is this?"

Sean's hearty laugh surprised her. He remained sitting but his whole body shuddered with his deep, gut-splitting laughter. She paused to watch him. His eyes were closed. His broad shoulders shook with the sound. The tension in her gut eased a bit turning everything inside pliant.

He opened his eyes, starting as if surprised to see her watching him. He cocked a brow and gave her a sly look. "I did warn ye."

Thomasina wiped her mouth with the back of her hand and smiled. A heartfelt smile. "Ye did."

"Ye should have listened to me."

"Yea." She raised her eyebrows in expectation. "Have ye had enough fun with me now?"

Too late she realized she'd not disguised her voice. She swallowed hard. She waited.

His smile faded like early morning fog. His face became serious. "Mayhap not. Is there more fun to be had with ye?"

The intimate scene closed in around her. All alone with a handsome stranger. A stranger who believed she was a boy. Surely there was no threat to her innocence here.

She cleared her throat and brushed off the seat of her pants. "Well, *I* think ye've teased me enough for one night." Her voice sounded very much like a boy now. "I'm for bed."

Thomasina glanced around and found the long, deer skin brat. She hesitated. If she were indeed a boy, would it seem odd for them to share a covering? Maybe not but she'd certainly feel odd sharing it with this man. Odd enough to not get a wink of sleep. Mayhap she'd wait to decide what to do. She had more pressing matters at present.

"I'll find myself a quiet spot and be back in a shake." She did not look back at Sean before heading off into the dark forest.

CHAPTER 3

Sean took a huge swallow of the bitter liquid, nearly choking himself. He shook his head at the heat working into his belly.

That was unexpected. And unwanted! When did he begin to pay attention to the fact that she was a female?

No doubt every time she forgot to disguise her voice. Or at the sight of her rounded bottom filling out the trews every time she bent over the fire. A fine sight. A mighty fine arse. She wanted to see to the fire? So be it. He'd even goaded her with disparaging comments about the small size of the flame, about it barely giving off any heat, about how he could do a much better job. She couldn't ignore that. Instead she kept working on it, adding twigs, poking it around. She'd been working on it for nigh on two hours. And he was rock hard.

It became more difficult to focus on treating her as the lad she pretended to be. She did a terrible job. She couldn't even alight from a horse properly.

I'm not a child.

That may sound like something a lad might say but not in answer to the opportunity to learn more swear words. By the time Sean turned ten and three, he could swear with the best of them. He'd also learned to spit fifteen feet. He laughed. Mayhap he should compete with her on that.

Sleeping arrangements may be a problem with only the one covering. It was a cool enough night. He could let her have it but would that seem awkward? A lad would expect no such treatment.

The rustling from the woods warned him of her return. Her cheeks were flushed and wisps of auburn hair had come loose, framing her face. He had to hold back the need to ask if all was well. He wouldn't ask if she were a lad.

"Aon scéal agat?"

Damn.

He couldn't stop himself but he refused to look at her. Just another glance. Her lips were red as if she'd been rubbing them. She must have gone back to the loch and washed herself. A huge damp spot on her tunic revealed far too much about what lay beneath. His breath caught. He looked away before he would see more.

"Yea." She fidgeted next to the brat.

He couldn't bring himself to see her sleep on the cold ground without a cover. "Go ahead and use the skin. I'm not for bed till later."

"Are ye certain?"

"Aye. I don't usually sleep much when I travel."

"Ye're not from here?"

Why did she have to keep talking to him?

"Just get ye to bed, youngling." He sounded harsh and a glance toward her revealed her hurt expression. "Enough talking now."

He closed his eyes but faced the fire. The fetching sight of one well-rounded breast and her taut nipple pressing against the rough material shot right to his groin.

"If ye're certain—"

"To bed!" Sean took another long sip and fought against the urge to look at her.

The sound of her movement was more than enough for him to visualize her standing near the fire, shaking the deer hide, wrapping it around herself—

"Are ye certain?"

He stood and headed into the forest without another word. She was killing him. A walk would do him good. Get his raging desires under control.

He returned a short time later to find her curled up, asleep, and turned away from the fire. The brat lay a few feet away as if she couldn't bear to take his only covering. That was not what a lad would do either.

"Stupid girl," Sean muttered under his breath before going to retrieve it.

He shook it out and stooped beside her. Her eyes were closed. Her breathing steady. Her fine arse poking out beneath her leine. A good, firm arse. Good to caress. Good to grab with both hands. Good to hold while he pumped into her.

He leaned in to peer further over her shoulder. With her hands tucked between her legs for warmth, her loose top bunched open. A good swell of cleavage confirming her breasts were just the right size. More than a handful was a waste.

His breath tightened. He mentally shook himself.

She mumbled in her sleep.

He covered her with the brat and stood. All properly covered now. He remained rooted to the ground unable to take his eyes off her. The gentle curve of her neck attracted his attention. The lobe of her small ear just visible beneath her thick hair. If he kissed her there, she'd surely moan.

"Sweet Jesus." Sean glanced toward heaven for some help. He forced his feet to move away, to the other side of the fire where he dropped onto the hard ground.

Sean needed a good swiving. He'd gone without satisfaction for too long, even turning away a few very eager lasses. Women always noticed him. They liked his large size—and there had never been a shortage of females. It had been that way since he'd first sprouted up before the other lads. And continued to grow. Some of his best curses were learned from the mouths of the women slaking themselves on his rod.

This time he'd been holding off until he could finally be with Brighit. He'd convinced himself that now she would accept him if only to avoid taking vows as a nun. Never did he believe she would have fallen for someone else. Tadhg had actually rolled his eyes when Sean explained he saved himself for Brighit. That had been the reason Sean offered his friend's treasured knife as collateral for the horse.

So now the first woman he encounters keeps setting him off like an untried lad. That had to be the reason for this urge to poke this particular female. Her unintentional offer to him had shot right to his balls. There was definitely more fun to be had with that one. He'd found himself considering the best plan for getting her out of those trews so he could pay homage to that tight arse and find what other treasures lay between her legs.

He snorted, his lips curled into a sneer. "Well that's not going to happen." He grabbed the skin and emptied its contents into his mouth. "Not ever."

Propping his head against the log, he stared into the fire. This was not a need he was about to get satisfied by some woman who, for whatever reason, dressed up like a lad. He'd go for a properly dressed, shapely woman. With breasts that hung like fruit. Like Brighit. Perhaps once he saw this one reunited with her brother, he'd find himself some willing wench.

The fog in his brain finally spread throughout his head and he slept.

It was the cold that awoke him. His body stiff from the hard ground and the frigid dampness working through his limbs. The fire glowed with its dying embers. He poked it around with a stick and tossed in the last few pieces of dried wood.

He glanced toward Tommy. She had not moved. Body warmth was not to be taken lightly. He crossed the camp and dropped behind her, lifting the long brat to cover himself as well.

Sean kept a discreet distance between them. The deer skin material did much to ward off the cold and he quickly drifted back to sleep.

In his dreams, a lovely woman with flowing brown hair rode behind him, astride his mount. His own horse, Hamish, so he must be in Eire. That would mean the woman would be Brighit. Her arms wrapped tightly around his middle. His hand covered hers but he found them ice cold. He tried to warm them, even bringing them to his mouth for a hot breath. They refused to heat up.

Was she dead?

He jumped down from Hamish and reached up to take the woman by her middle. It wasn't Brighit. Someone he'd never seen before. She had dark brows arching over fetching green eyes. Her smile looked sad and he knew he had to get her warm or she would surely die. He held her against him. She molded into the contours of his arms, pressing her small form against his chest.

"I canna get warm," she said.

He stroked her silky hair down her back. "Shh."

His hand grazed her from crown to buttocks. A firm, round buttocks. "Mmm, ye're cold everywhere."

"What are ye doing?"

The woman suddenly pulled away from him. Her expression spoke of accusations he didn't understand.

He opened his eyes. His hands were tucked between his knees and his teeth chattered.

"What are ye doing?" The woman dressed as a lad.

"Trying to sleep." Exhaustion pulled at him. The darkness around them indicated sunrise was still a long way off. "Let me sleep."

"Ye need not share yer cloak."

Tommy sat beside him, her hair a mess around her shoulders, her tunic askew, and eyes that were shooting arrows at him.

"I decided I did. Go back to sleep."

"I'm not comfortable like this I... usually sleep alone. Ye're too close."

He glared at her. "I dunna bother young boys. Go back to sleep and let me do the same."

"I dinna—"

She sounded like a girl again.

"I dinna say ye did."

And now she sounded like a girl pretending to be a boy.

"Argh!" Sean stood up, dropping the brat on her. "Here! Have the damned thing."

He went to the fire and dug around hoping for some flames.

"I dunna want it." She threw the covering toward him. It nearly landed in the fire.

Resentment shot through his gut like a knife blade. Sean clenched his teeth holding back his angry retort but allowed his expression to speak for him when he faced her. Boys did not throw items around a fire. Boys did not complain about having someone sleeping too close. Boys took what they were offered and shut up about it.

"I think ye need yer arse slapped but good."

Her eyes widened, she stepped back, and gasped as if he were about to redden her bottom at that very moment. He turned away from her and toward the fire. "Give me any more trouble and I'll see to it myself."

From the sound of the movements, *Tommy* must have laid back down. A quick glance told him she'd rolled away from him. Unexpectedly, she stood back up. He turned away, feigning little interest. She went to retrieve the brat, covered herself with it, and turned away from the fire again.

Sean laughed quietly. Quite a spitfire. If he'd had more time, she might be an interesting puzzle to work out. Who she was and why she dressed like a boy. And why wasn't she married yet? But he had duties of his own. Once he returned the horse and had Tadhg's knife back in hand, he didn't care what she did with the horse.

Tadhg had left Eire in a hurry to protect Brighit, who, it turned out, didn't need his help. He'd left a mess behind, barely enough food for the clan to make it through winter. Now he chose to stay behind and help the Normans, sending Sean on ahead to see to everything. Not Tadhg's finest hour and certainly not anything Sean wanted to take on.

Calum would make it over to Eire before him, making his way along the coast to Drogheda. He was a good man. Very level-headed. Tadhg had arranged for food from the neighboring O'Brien and Calum would be there to help manage the stores. Sean wasn't really needed for any of that. He'd only be needed for defense. Clans didn't attack during winter months.

Sean wasn't good with words. It wasn't worth the effort. Maybe that's what Brighit had against him. He wasn't smooth like her brother, Tadhg. All the MacNaughtons had that polished way about them.

Sean was a man of action. And if muscle and force were needed, even better. It worked best for him. He saw no reason to change that, especially now since the love of his life had thrown him over for another.

That one—Sir Peter of Normandy—seemed polished as well. He knew the right words to say. Even had the calmness to listen rather than react. Nothing like Sean. If that's what Brighit had looked for in a husband, it was a good thing they hadn't married. His passion ran too deep, took over too often, to wait around for things to happen.

"Good riddance to ye, Brighit." Sean mumbled the words aloud perhaps hoping to rid her from his mind by the power of his declaration. His eyes soon drifted closed and he was again asleep. A peaceful sleep not disturbed by dreams and beautiful women that needed his help.

Bleary-eyed, Thomasina stumbled through the woods with an urgent need to see to nature's call. Damn trews. Untie this. Yank at that. Shimmy this down. Ah, to be in a dress again. She never thought she'd be thinking that.

The birds had awoken her with their incessant chatter and followed her, growing even louder, as she'd followed the path. Another thing she didn't have in the cave—the loud sound of nature. Why did she ever leave there?

"Tommy," Sean bellowed from the camp.

He'd been fast asleep, snoring even, when she'd awoken.

"Tommy!" He moved closer and his tone sounded urgent. She fumbled with the foreign clothing.

"I'll be back anon," she said over her shoulder.

She pulled at the tie. Damn thing was wet. How did men manage this? Oh that's right. Different appendages.

"Where have ye gone to?"

"I am right here." She sounded irritated. Good. She tried again to loop the damp material only to find her leine had not cleared the top of her trews. Damn, but she'd never complain about a dress again. "Give me one moment."

The rustling of the trees indicated he was just behind her.

"Wait!" She turned away from the sounds, dropping her trews to yank the twisted top out.

What sounded suspiciously like a groan of appreciation sounded in her ears. With trembling hands, she fought to right her clothing and refused to acknowledge what may have just happened. With a final tug on the bow at her waist, she stiffened her shoulders and took a deep breath before facing him.

Finding his back to her was a surprise. He looked as if he were giving her privacy until she recognized the telltale trickle of water. Sean was urinating.

"Sorry to interrupt ye, lad." His voice sounded strained. "I could not find the horse—"

She clasped her hand over her mouth to cover her gasp.

"—and my first reaction was that ye'd taken yer horse and left me here."

He turned to face her. Everything thankfully put back in its place. He smiled.

"Most happy to see ye had nae such ideas."

She forced her head left then right. "Nae such idea."

Sean ran his eyes over her in that way that set her heart to fluttering. She swallowed hard but refused to confirm all was decently covered. It had to be. His expression when his eyes returned to her face said as much.

"Sorry to interrupt ye," he said.

"Nae problem. I was—" What was it her brother always said? "—just finishing up."

Sean pressed his lips into a lopsided grin. "Shall we break our fast before we head off?"

He said it like a question but his large, tanned hand directing her to precede him down the path certainly left her without an option. With Sean following close behind, she returned to the camp, thanking God in heaven that her nakedness had not been seen by this man. He was quite disturbing enough without him having that knowledge of her.

CHAPTER 4

The lass moved about the fire with deliberation. Sean would have liked to beg her to stop. Would have liked to beg her to sit and remain seated. Would have liked to beg to not have wandered down the path behind her and not seen the flash of silky pale flesh that lay hidden beneath. But he had.

With every poke and jab at the flames, her clothing molded over that flawless buttocks. What had started out as a jest—a jest? Perhaps in his own mind—was now sheer torture. Beyond having any right to demand she stop now, it seemed a just punishment for his transgression. And the painful throbbing in his groin? His penance.

When she glanced his way, she hesitated before offering him the tea as if sensing his inner turmoil.

"Nae thank ye." He stopped her before she could fully extend the cup to him. He didn't dare take the chance of touching her soft skin.

He watched her eat. Like a girl. Far too clean. Boys did not care if their hands were dirty before, during, or after they ate. He wanted to tell her to work harder at pretending to be a boy. To yell it at her. He wished she was better at it instead of all these constant reminders.

But no. Every graceful movement, every brushing off of her bottom at standing, every dainty swipe of the stray hairs from her face, every single morsel passing her full, red lips screamed she was a girl in boy's clothing.

"Ye're quite effeminate. Has anyone ever told ye that?"

He'd have liked to call the words back. The last thing he needed was for her to come clean with some confession. If she started dressing like a girl, he'd never be able to keep his hands off her.

"I have been told that. I'm sorry if that offends ye."

"It will make it hard when we reach the sea. Some of the men there have been a long time on the ocean. Some have been a long time without a woman. Even a boy who only looks like a girl may help ease their need."

"But how—"

"Do not ask." Her delectable bottom came to his mind. "Just try to stop being so… so womanly."

Tommy glanced away from the fire but he could see the shimmer of tears.

Damn. Don't go confessing to me now.

He stood abruptly. "Well, ye best pack up and we'll get started."

He hoped to intercept anything she might decide to share.

She cleared her throat and stood as well.

Oh damn.

"How long will it take us?" she asked.

Sean exhaled his relief but he knew it could be just a matter of time before she may decide to make her confession. Then what? He preferred the pretending. Without the pretense, he traveled with a beautiful, desirable woman. He stomped about the small area picking up this and that.

"Canna be fast enough for me," he said.

He shook out the soft deer hide, rolled it up, then carried it to the horse. He tied it behind the saddle followed by his shield. The animal had been fed and watered and seemed eager to be gone. He knew the feeling. The idea of having *Tommy* pressed against his back, especially now that he knew exactly what lay beneath, rode him hard.

Maybe a little distance would help the situation. "Can ye fill the water skins?"

She didn't move. Out of the corner of his eye, he noticed she squared her shoulders and tipped her head back. All the signs of preparing for an argument.

"Never mind. I'll see to it." He yanked at the skins attached to the saddle but refused to look her in the face. He took two steps—

"I have done nothing to deserve such poor treatment from ye."

Not quick enough. *Poor treatment?*

Well, if that didn't sound like something a woman would say. She would have to promise not to talk when they were in the village.

"Please!" In that one word, she managed to convey the gut-wrenching emotion of one begging for mercy from an unjust punishment.

Sean pivoted to face her. He blew an exasperated breath and pressed his lips together not even trying to hide his anger. "Are ye joking?"

Her shoulders rounded. She shook her head.

"I was on my way to the village yesterday. A happy man. Happy to be seeing an end to this damnable trip. And I would have made it to the boat by today. My companion certainly will. He'll soon be back in Eire. On his way to his home. His family. Me? Nae. I'm still here. I had expected to be able to make it with him. Certainly. After all I'd rightfully paid for the use of a horse that could see me there. But ye," he jabbed his finger toward her, "had other ideas. Unbeknownst to me, my horse was stolen from some sap of a boy who thought to take it back. Probably the first manly act of yer life."

The horse properly saddled, the skins still not full, Sean leapt onto its back.

"Give me yer hand now and get on this horse like a proper lad or I swear I will leave ye behind."

Tommy moved at lightning speed to grab the last few items and reach up to him. Sean yanked at her arm knowing full-well such treatment would probably leave her shoulder sore. He rode to the loch, slid off the horse and filled the water skins himself.

Now ready to travel, he climbed onto the horse and headed back to the trail leading down the hill. Tommy's small hands grasped at his sides before she slammed against his back, her arms wrapped around his middle, holding on for dear life. He refused to acknowledge his body's reaction.

The trees raced past, mimicking the blood coursing through his veins. It felt good to be on his way. It felt good to have this little bit of release. It felt good to be getting closer to his home. The steady pounding of the horse's hooves reverberated through him. The repetition of the weightless lift then slamming down eased his tension. One with the animal. This trip would be a memory soon enough.

The wide path they followed steepened then crisscrossed the mountain. It might ease the steepness but it also increased the distance. The miles dragged by. Sean had no patience for this and spoke little, alternating between a quick trot and a slow gallop. Best left to his thoughts, he was constantly reminded he was not alone by the ceaseless shifting behind him.

"Are ye unable to sit still?"

The lass cleared her throat. "I need to take a piss."

Sean swallowed down the laugh that nearly erupted. At least she tried to sound like a lad. He eased the horse into a stop, trying to keep the smile from his face.

Tommy rocked behind him but didn't move to jump down.

"What are ye waiting for?" Sean spoke over his shoulder to avoid looking directly at her.

"Oh." She shifted first to the left then to the right. When she smashed her chest against him and dropped her legs over the side, he understood why. She was apparently trying to jump down without grabbing at him for assistance. She immediately ran off to the woods.

Her breasts were a problem. A problem to his focus because he couldn't stop thinking about them. About caressing them. About suckling them. About crushing them against him as he impaled her with his rod that seemed no longer capable of becoming flaccid. No. Not a problem as far as lusting after her went.

They were, however, a constant warning of the dangers they would face when they arrived in the village. With every awkward jolt or sudden shift, he remembered. There would be no call for her to ride behind anyone else. Perhaps he worried unnecessarily. If he could set his lust aside and see her as others might...

When she returned a short while later, a big smile of relief on her comely face, he knew he worried with good reason. She was lovely when she smiled.

"Do ye always smile so after taking a piss?" He used his most belittling tone.

Her crestfallen face tugged at his heart. It was for her own good. He strengthened his resolve.

"Ye must have been raised by a gaggle of women." Perhaps reminding her of the roll she needed to play would help her. "But ye mentioned a brother. And a father?"

Her eyes turned dark. "Yea. I have one."

She grabbed at the arm he extended and managed to resume her seat in one, swift movement.

"I'm impressed."

She made a noise that reminded him of a growl. He urged his horse on. The sun was high in the sky when he decided to rest. Sean found an open field beside a brook that offered the perfect spot. He jumped down beside the water leaving the horse, and Tommy, to fend for themselves.

When he returned a short while later, Tommy didn't hear his return. She spoke to her horse. He paused a short distance away.

"We'll be home before ye ken it, Daisy, and then I willna let ye out of my sight."

Perhaps she wasn't lying about her horse being stolen—no, taken without permission.

"...surely Father will see he needs to be more particular with who he hands me off to. Look at how he treated ye! Lose ye at the first game of chance, did he? Is that what happened? Would he do any more with me?"

"And how is yer horse at conversing?" Sean continued toward the horse.

Tommy took a step away, her cheeks reddening but she said nothing. Damn. She needed to hide her emotions.

"Did I hear ye call her Daisy? What an awful name for such a fine animal." He took the horse's reins, standing a few feet from Tommy. "Did yer sister name her?"

A frown flashed across her face. "Ah, yea. My older sister. I... I let her name my horse. She likes flowers. Girls. Ye ken."

"Hmm, yea, I ken." His mouth tightened. "And yer brother?"

"Nae, he does not like flowers."

Sean raised an eyebrow. Was she being funny now? "I asked what yer brother was like? Does he browbeat ye?"

"Browbeat me?"

"Bully ye? Boss ye about? Get his kicks at yer expense? Browbeat ye."

"Nae! Why would ye ask that?"

"Ye're very… girly. I wondered if mayhap he pushed ye around a lot. Making ye feel timid or afeared all the time."

She seemed to freeze. Not a muscle twitched. Her eyes never leaving his. The intensity of that gaze worked its way into him, rippling through his arms, down to his chest, and lastly, down to his groin. He had an overwhelming urge to take her into his arms. To feel her tight up against him. His breathing slowed. Deep. Slow. Breaths. A more powerful reaction he could not remember. He gritted his teeth.

"My apologies for not being man enough for ye. I am young yet and have time to learn to be the bully I suppose I am expected to become. Saying mean things to people. Standing close enough to intimidate so they will cower beneath me. Perhaps I'll even grow a bit to help me do just that. For now, I try to stay clear of brutish men unless I have a need for them. Then I am forced to put up with their behavior and pray that our time together will end sooner rather than later. Are we ready to continue? I hoped to be rid of ye by nightfall."

When she finally turned away, Sean blew out a slow breath. Her passion, albeit *anger*, was all powerful. He yearned to unleash it and see where it would go. He would accept her fists pounding against his chest if she wanted anger. And he would accept her grinding against him as she rode him hard to her pleasure if she wanted passion. This was not an ideal situation either way. He couldn't get to town fast enough.

She grasped the saddle and pulled herself onto the back of her mount in one smooth motion. If not for that fetching backside, he would have taken her for a lad without any problem. How would she react if he ran his hand up her thighs to grasp her bottom? Would it be anger or lust? He watched her a moment longer but she remained stiff backed, facing front, and refused to meet his gaze. Anger for certain. Outrage more than likely. He shrugged then mounted in front of her.

The horse skittered. Sean could feel the tension as well. Tommy's breathing accelerated, her cheeks had been flushed, but no sign of tears. No. She was angry with him for his insults. He had his reasons. Reasons she was unaware as of yet. He hoped to keep it that way.

Thomasina kept her head averted and waited until the last possible moment to wrap her arms around the arrogant bastard's middle. She'd swear he enjoyed the faster speeds just so she had to hold on tight. No doubt it made him feel all powerful.

The intimate contact grated on her nerves. Heat emanated from him. And he was so broad that when she wrapped her arms around him, her face was drawn up against him. If it had been her brother, who wasn't nearly so broad, she would have rested her head against his back so she could be more comfortable. At present, her neck pained from the strain of holding herself up away. She was already too close. Close enough to smell his musky, manly scent.

His insults were getting hard to take. Admittedly, men teased each other. This man seemed different. This man meant to do harm. This man wanted to break her. Of course he didn't realize she wasn't a boy. Her life would be so much easier if she were a boy. Her father wouldn't have used her as payment for a debt. She'd be married and bedded by some lecherous old man by now if she hadn't snuck off. She was a person, not property. Her brother would be able to talk sense into their father and get her out of this mess. He always did.

The village came into view. A few huts scattered on either side of the road that led to the sea. A large boat made its way from the shore.

"Damn." Sean muttered under his breath and jumped down. He yanked the lead on the horse without allowing her a chance to get down.

"What—" She coughed. "What are ye about?"

The big man didn't even glance at her. His knuckles were white where he clenched the rein. "Ye're to be seen and not heard. Put a lock on it."

Thomasina, the woman, dropped her jaw ready to let lose a tirade but Tommy, the lad, slammed it shut. "Yea, sir."

Sean stumbled slightly. She thought he was going to turn towards her but then he squared his broad shoulders. She had the sneaking suspicion he stopped himself from glancing back at her. No. That was silly.

They continued away from the houses but Thomasina decided she would listen to his order. For now. Nestled within the shelter of the trees, Sean halted the horse and secured his sword at his belt. He faced her with a stern visage. One of those ye're-not-going-to-like-what-I-have-to-say looks. He crossed his arms. A rock settled in her stomach. This was not going to be good.

Sean paused. "Ye stink."

She frowned then tried to sniff without being obvious to see if she could smell anything. *His scent* was the only thing she could pick up.

His cheek twitched. "I will not be kicked out of the only establishment here that will provide food because my companion offends the others with his odor."

He reached toward the bag that hung beside Thomasina's leg. When he brushed her knee, he jerked his hand away. She shifted her leg further back to give him access. He glanced at the widened juncture of her legs then up at her face. His eyes were dark. His lips parted.

"I have some things in my bag ye might be able to use to… prepare yerself to be in a room full of other *brutish* men. Be quick about it."

Sean strode away, stiff backed. She jumped off the horse landing squarely on her feet then smiled. If a lad can learn how to get off a horse without help, so could she. She reached into the bag. A rolled up piece of vellum. A leine. A tunic. A strip of leather. A small hatchet. A swath of course material. She glanced over the horse's back to where Sean had gone but saw nothing. The material would suit for binding herself. Yanking her top off, she quickly worked the material around her, pulling it tight before tucking it under itself. She ran her hands over her chest. Smooth. Perfect.

A rustling grew closer and she pulled the tunic over her head, being certain to tuck her long, auburn braid inside. Sean's scent wafted up to her. Her eyes drifted closed. It set her heart to racing. Not all together unpleasant. Earthy. It seemed decadent to be surrounded by his aroma.

"I dinna promise ye'd have all day to do it."

She jumped at his voice, her eyes flying open.

Sean searched her face before running his glance over her clothing. She'd swear he paused at her breasts, glancing left then right. No. It must be her imagination. Then he sniffed, moving closer even. He nodded. "Might want to roll the sleeves up. 'Tis quite a bit too large."

He rummaged inside the bag and tossed her the strip of leather. "Ye can use that to tie up the waist."

She belted the leather with a knot. Sean removed a smaller sack that had been hidden along the saddle and withdrew a single coin. His eyes remained on her as he hung the pouch behind his scabbard at his belt. He grabbed the horse's lead and they walked toward the largest of the thatch-covered buildings. A group of swarthy men gathered outside the entrance. Sea men. Sean tipped his head in acknowledgment, secured the horse, then shoved Thomasina none too gently ahead of him.

"Sit there and dunna get up." He pointed to the table tucked in the far corner of the room.

Thomasina dropped onto the bench that faced away from the door, biting her lip to keep from responding. With narrowed eyes, she watched the arrogant man swagger to the front trestle beside the fire. An open door beyond revealed the larger, cooking fire out back being seen to by an older couple. The man noticed Sean and came inside.

The small room had several tables with benches. The area was darkening fast with sunset. A single lighted lamp hung at the door. It must be more important to see who came and went than what the food looked like. The fire cast strange shadows about the room and the others present. Six men in all. She faced ahead of her, sitting in near total darkness. When she glanced back at Sean, he and the other man were gone.

Her stomach clenched. She searched the area again. More men were gathering outside. Their laughter carried and she recognized the signs of overindulgence. They were all drunk. She ducked low, hunching forward, trying to avoid being noticed. A serving lass brought her a wooden mug of cider then lit the iron lamp above her.

"Th—" Thomasina cleared her throat. "Thank ye."

The girl came in closer then frowned. "Is there anything else you'd like?"

Thomasina drew back at her angry tone. "Nae."

"Good!" The redhead glanced around then lowered her voice. "I don't expect any trouble from you. Do you hear?"

Thomasina had no idea what she was talking about. "Yea. Nae trouble."

"This is my place." She spoke in a raspy tone as she pointed to her chest with her thumb. She leaned forward, her gown opening up for a clear view of her feminine assets. "If I see you so much as bat your eyes at any of these men, you won't make it to wherever 'tis you're going. Understand?"

Thomasina did not. She nodded her head. "Nae trouble."

The lass smirked before walking away to light the lamp opposite. The men across the room followed her with their eyes. The heavier one rubbed at his gray-whiskered chin.

"The wares are good enough I'm thinking."

The two laughed and slammed their mugs together. Fear flooded Thomasina's chest. That girl recognized her as a woman. She pressed back into the shadows. How? Sean dropped down opposite her.

"What's wrong? Ye look as if ye've seen the devil himself."

She let out a sigh of relief which quickly shifted to panic. If it was obvious to that woman, maybe Sean knew as well. She shook her head.

Sean's eyes rounded and he leaned in closer. "Are ye going to be sick?"

She shook her head more quickly. She had to get out of here. Where could she go?

"Nae." She stood up, all her thoughts scattering except for one. She had to get away from this place. Now.

"Sit."

"Nae. Ye dunna understand—" Or maybe he did. Earlier comments reminding her to behave like a boy. His knuckles grazing her breast when he shoved her. The way he watched her by the fire. She narrowed her eyes. "Ye ken dunna ye?"

Sean glanced over his shoulder, grabbing her hand. "Sit down. Ye're calling attention to yerself."

Her head shook violently. "Nae."

He held her fast when she attempted to loosen his grip. "Sit, *Tommy*. Now."

"I have to leave." Her voice tight.

"Sit down."

Others were glancing toward them.

"I told ye what type of men are here." A warning tone. "If anyone else suspects, 'tis yer own doing. Not mine."

Sean released his hold of her. Her knees shook. Thomasina slowly sat down. She reached for her mug. Her hands shook. She had to escape but she didn't know where to go. The men who had been outside were coming into the room, filling up all the empty tables, standing along the walls, blocking the exit. She was overwhelmed by the sudden sense that danger surrounded her.

Sean's large, warm hand covered hers. "Look at me."

She jerked her eyes back to his warm eyes, rounded with compassion contradicting his demanding tone.

"Ye'll be fine." He smiled, a reassuring smile meant to alleviate her fears.

That's it? No question? No demand for answers? He knew!

"How long have ye known?" When they'd lain together? Her face heated. He'd known right from the start. "Why? Why dinna ye confront me?"

He narrowed his eyes, assessing her. "Why? I cared only that ye dinna get caught."

A few men just settling down next to them glanced at their hands. One man poked at the other, directing him with his head. They exchanged knowing smiles.

Thomasina's breath quickened. She withdrew her hand, immediately missing his warmth, and placed it in her lap.

Sean sat up straighter. He nodded to the men beside them then turned back to her. He put his hand to his mouth as if to rub his lips. He said, "Now they think I like boys."

She knew she looked shocked but she couldn't seem to stop herself.

Then the reality of what he told her seeped through her fear-saturated mind. "They believe I am a boy?"

"Why would they not?"

She glanced around. Everyone else had lost interest in her. No one else seemed overly concerned. "So they dunna ken?"

"Ye're doing a fine job. Nae one else knows."

"The serving lady. She knew."

"She was not a lady."

"Well, I ken that but she… she threatened me."

He smirked, glancing down into his own mug before facing her. "I imagine she saw ye as a threat to her business."

Thomasina's jaw nearly dropped when she understood his meaning.

Sean handed her his cup. "Drink this. Ye'll feel better."

She obliged him. Not one for drinking anything stronger than cider, the liquid went down surprisingly easy.

"Thank ye."

He smiled at her. An understanding smile. Thomasina would have sworn he hadn't an understanding bone in his body. Mayhap there was more to the man than brawn and bullying.

Sean tensed and shifted forward in his seat. He seemed transfixed by something just beyond her. His smile shifted to one of appreciation. When Thomasina looked over her shoulder, she saw the red-haired woman coming toward the table. Her hips swaying with every step. Her gaze fixed on Sean. She placed the wooden plate complete with crusted bread covered with an aromatic broth and a hunk of meat betwixt them on the table, never taking her eyes off him.

Sean smiled, his gaze seductively surveying her wares. Tension coiled in Thomasina's gut. She had the overwhelming urge to scratch the woman's eyes out.

"Anything else you see that you'd like?" Her voice was honey sweet now.

Thomasina clenched her hands so tightly that her nails dug into her palms.

"Not yet." Sean's white teeth were in sharp contrast to his dark beard when he gave her a lopsided grin. "Dunna stray far."

The wench leaned forward. The same technique she'd used on Thomasina but for a different reason. Sean's smile widened at the display of her womanly attributes.

"I will be very near, ready to give you *whatever* you want."

She dipped her shoulder and turned to leave. Anger uncoiled from Thomasina's belly like a snake. Something she couldn't control. She stuck her foot out. The redhead tripped and nearly fell except for the man at the next table who caught her.

"Well then. What have we here?" he said.

The redhead struggled to regain her composure. "Get your hands off me."

The glare Thomasina received was quite gratifying. Where did she come off flirting with her... companion? When Thomasina finally turned back to Sean, her smug smile dropped. His gimlet eye said it all. She lowered her gaze. She prayed he wouldn't ask her why she did that. She wouldn't know what to answer.

"Apologies." She hadn't meant to anger him.

"Methinks ye're too much." Sean took a long pull on his mead then stood. "I need something stronger." He grabbed the hunk of meat as if just realizing his hunger for the food. "Eat. Stay seated. And try not to call attention to yerself."

If she hadn't been starving, eating the food that woman brought over would be the last thing she would do. But she wasn't the cook. Just the serving wench... and bedding wench. Thomasina glanced behind to see Sean talking to a little man in a dark cape. A shiver went down her spine. The short man stood with his legs parted as if ready to withstand anyone knocking him down. His arrogant tone carried even with all the noise around her. Sean didn't look all that interested.

So be it. Let him stay over there and maybe she could get a little peace. When she reached for the bread, his scent wafted up from her tunic. Mayhap not so much peace.

CHAPTER 5

"*I* am called Ivan."

Sean hesitated before switching his food to the other hand and accepting the extended arm. "Sean."

"Ah, a good Eire man. I am from across the sea as well. Not a lot of us around here." He sipped his drink and glanced around the room. "And far too many Normans."

Sean finished off his meal and glanced around. "Are there Normans here?"

The man looked at him as if he had two heads. "Enough."

Sean didn't care for the topic of Normans and remained silent.

"One is too many!" Ivan laughed at his own joke and slapped Sean on the back.

Sean unclenched his fist to throw back his drink. Stronger than the mead, it went down smooth. Helping himself to the clay jug, he poured himself more. Things were taking a turn for the worse with *Tommy*. The sooner he was done with her, the better. The sight of the curragh making its way back home had set him in a foul mood.

Ivan watched him with an expectant look. "I said one Norman is too many. Do you not agree?"

Sean knew of one Norman who was definitely too many. "Yea."

Why not agree? Sean could put up a pretense as well as the next man. He rubbed his eyes. The memory of Brighit in that bastard's arms. And the morning after the bedding, she'd looked… sated and very contented. The liquid burned this time.

"Eh?" Ivan was bent on conversing. "God's teeth! They think they own the world."

Sean wanted the man to stop talking to him. He'd made a straight line for him and there'd been no escape. "Ivan? What say we talk later?"

Sean lifted the jug and headed to the door then realized he couldn't very well leave his little pretend lad unprotected. The last thing he'd wanted to do was play escort and God help him, not to a female. Game of chance? Was that how she'd lost the animal? Someone her sire had handed her off to. So was she betrothed now or not?

Another woman might have gone along with whatever her father said, obediently marrying and living a miserable life. Not Thomasina. She dresses up like a lad and goes off to collect her horse. She did have courage… and an arse as pale as sheepskin bleaching in the sun. That memory shot to his groin.

He surveyed the room until his eyes found the one he sought. When the redhead glanced his way, he winked. She smiled and started making her way toward him. He leaned beside the door and waited. Tommy's head barely visible. The room was crowded with men drinking and looking for a little relaxation. He preferred to dip his wick before the others had a chance at her.

"Time away from your little friend?" She placed her hand on his chest. Her eyes widened. "My you are a broad one."

"What? Oh. Yea." Sean leaned forward and slid his fingers down the side of her head. Her hair was not as soft as it looked. She moved in closer, her body nearly touching him. She smelled of onions.

"Is there ought else you'd like to be touching?" Her voice was throaty.

"Yea." The alcohol was deadening any objections. He tunneled his fingers beneath her hair. "I'd like to be doing more than touching though."

"Mmm, as would I." She glanced around and whispered, "Mayhap—"

"Nell!" A loud voice bellowed and the woman jumped.

Sean held her gaze, his eyebrows raised. "Nell, I presume?"

She tipped her head. "I need to see to the serving of the food."

Sean watched her walk away. His cock was rock hard. Perhaps a walk outside. Uh. No. His ward. He glanced over at the lass dressed like a lad and finished off the bottle. What was the truth? Maybe she enjoyed this little pretense. Maybe she'd always wanted to be a boy so she dressed like one, acted like one, and probably pissed like one. He laughed aloud. Then again she wasn't very good at the acting part. No. Hands her off to? What to hell does that mean?

He hadn't noticed Ivan coming toward him again but there he was beside him, a horn of mead in his hand.

"Yup. A lot goes on here. Even the sounds of their lousy voices set me off."

The man glanced around the room. He feigned a casual interest but Sean wasn't fooled. The tightness of his grip. The intense stare whenever he looked at Sean. This man had some sort of agenda.

"Ye hate Normans."

"Aye. I do." Ivan glanced around before continuing. "This was not the way of it before, you know."

"Before?"

"Before those Normans came. The sound of their rotten voices filling the room. It used to be the sweet sound of..."

Sean waited for him to continue.

"Un-Normans." The man guffawed, bending over to slap his knee. He glanced at Sean and his ugly face curled into an uglier frown. "Thought you'd be more wary what with you being from Eire and all."

"Wary? Go back home if ye do not care for the Normans."

Ivan's face darkened. "It will not be long before they cross the sea and crush us, as well!"

Sean glanced around. More than half the men were Normans and their voices did carry. That also meant there were plenty here that weren't Normans.

"I dunna look for trouble. I have plenty of my own."

"You don't look like a stupid man, Sean." Ivan took a wary step back. "You look like a man that protects what's your own and does not care for others taking it from you."

A punch to the gut couldn't have been more soundly felt. This man was trouble and he egged him on. Sean took a deep cleansing breath. A man of action but it was action of his own choosing.

"Every Eire man would look out for his own. Talk like yers is trouble." He started to move away but Ivan grabbed him with an iron fist. Sean narrowed his eyes and moved in close to the man's face. "Either release my arm or ye'll be parting with that hand."

Ivan released Sean as if he'd been burned. He held his hand up in a display of contrition. "My apologies, man. I get a little excited."

"Yea." With a tight jaw, Sean stepped further into the room and away from the little man. Alarm bells sounded when the bald man moved to stand beside Tommy's table. Sean crossed to her in six strides, his hand pulling at the hilt of his sword.

"And what are ye about, youngling? Are ye up to nae good?" The bald man slurred his words and seemed to have a difficult time standing upright.

Sean breathed again, releasing the sword. The petrified look on Tommy's face tightened his gut. With a firm hand on the man's shoulder, Sean yanked him away from the table. The man stumbled back, cursing, as he tried to get his feet beneath him. The room became silent. All eyes were on them.

They did not need this type of attention. He took a protective step toward the table. "My companion prefers to be left alone while he's eating. That would mean ye."

"Me?" He brushed off his tunic and adjusted it.

Sean stepped back. He felt a surprisingly keen sense of disappointment at the other man's lack of offense. A fight now would have been enjoyable. Help to ease his tension. Then again, that would put Tommy in harm's way, exposing her for the tempting female that she was.

Tommy looked away as if trying to ignore the man who again teetered closer as if insisting on conversing with her.

Sean shoved the man away. "Back away!"

Ivan helped the bald man to stand. "What is amiss?"

"This man took offense at me conversing with his companion," the bald man said, again righting his clothing.

Ivan glanced toward Tommy but Sean stepped in to block his view.

"He doesn't want you talking to the lad?" Ivan asked.

"S'pose not." The bald man scratched at his jaw. "Don't ken why not. Ye?"

The sides of Ivan's mouth dropped down and he shook his head. "Damned if I know."

Once the two walked away without incident, the room quickly filled with the sound of men continuing in their own conversation. Sean turned back toward the table. Both Tommy's food and drink were gone. He caught a glimpse of the serving wench moving among the ever growing crowd of hungry men.

"More drink here." Sean raised his hand, speaking loudly over the din in the room. She nodded but when she reached for the stronger brew, he waved his hand. "Nae. The cider."

Nell paused as if confused. He gestured toward Tommy's cup. She gave an exasperated sigh. She brought it to the table amidst raucous hollers and suggestive slaps. She all but slammed it on the table, sloshing the liquid, her eyes boring into Tommy.

"Here. It. Is."

Tommy still had her eyes averted.

"Nae. NAE! Ye pour the drink here, dunna ye?" Damn, why was she being so miserable to Tommy?

Nell gave him a sideway glance and smirked. "Well, if you want your little *lad* to have more to drink, then I think you best be pouring it yourself."

When she would have sauntered off in a huff, Sean placed his hand on her arm, then smiled. "Thank ye, Nell."

She batted her eyes at him, her lips curling into a suggestive little bow as if just now remembering her own interest in him.

"Ye need not find me after yer done serving." His nostrils flared. His jaw tight. "I doubt I'd get any satisfaction now that I see how ye treat yer customers."

Nell's eyes widened in direct proportion to the dropping of her jaw. The loud gasp echoed back at them. It took Sean a moment to realize Tommy made the sound. He gave her a quick glance. Her green eyes were round with accusation and anger and she looked at *him*. Confusion clouded Sean's mind as he ran over what had just happened. He blew an exasperated breath.

Sean spoke in a loud voice. "I'll pay my bill and be gone."

The dark brows of the owner dipped into a dangerous frown. Nell scurried over to him, mouthing her defense before she'd even reached him. There was some satisfaction in that. The eyes now turned toward him narrowed with suspicion. He knew the look. They were seeing him as a troublemaker. Sean preferred to have done something worthy of the moniker.

When he reached for Tommy's arm, she jerked it away and stood. He shot her a disparaging frown and pulled her ahead of him, urging her toward the door but staying close. The owner's expression transformed with a brilliant smile for Sean when his gold coin appeared.

"Sorry for any misunderstanding."

Sean nodded. This was the only place in town that offered rooms so he knew he had to be accepting of the apology. "I think that will cover the room upstairs as well?"

"For one night. With two others."

"Nae. Nae one else. That's a gold coin."

The owner seemed to consider his offer. "A pallet to yourself and two on the floor."

"Nae. Nae one else in the room." Sean hated this part. It grated his nerves. He should get three rooms and food for a week with that gold.

"Done." The owner grabbed the coin.

"What bug is up yer arse?" Sean spoke through gritted teeth once they were done paying and outside again.

"Ye embarrassed—" She glanced around then turned so that her back was to the inn before she continued. "Ye embarrassed me by acting like that. Nae lad would get served there."

He halted mid-stride. That's what she was angry about? It was a very good thing he'd be rid of her soon. This female's thinking was beyond his ability to understand. He picked up his pace to pass her, leaving her behind to catch up.

"We need to find yer brother. Now!"

With a hurried gait, Sean led the way to the blacksmith's hut.

"Why are ye going here?" Tommy struggled to keep up with him.

He didn't care. "I need to collect the knife."

"This is where ye found Daisy?"

Daisy! What a damn stupid name for a horse. "The same."

"He's going to take her back then."

He jerked around to face her. "Stop acting like a girl, damn it."

"Ye said I was doing fine!"

"Then ye opened yer damn mouth!"

He continued on and she ran to catch up with him.

"He'll want my horse back." She hissed the words.

"Not when he realizes it was stolen from ye."

Tommy's doubt-filled expression gave him pause but too late. A barrel-chested man bent over a horse hoof glanced up at Sean. Recognition flashed across his face.

"Ah, so ye remember me?" Sean planted himself before the man. "Now why do ye suppose I'm getting a strange feeling that ye ken something is amiss?"

"I don't know what you're talking about." Head down, the man scraped the dirt with an iron pick. "You'll have to come back on the morrow. I'm closed."

Sean waited until the man looked up at him. He shook his head. "Now."

The man huffed and stood, his expression a mask of annoyance. He glanced over at Tommy. "Looking for a mount?"

"Methinks ye ken I've already had a mount from ye."

He squinted and looked as if he were trying to remember. "No. I do not remember you."

"Well, ye took my coin and my knife without hesitation. And then ye gave me a stolen horse."

"Stolen? No. All my horses are from the area."

Tommy moved in closer, put her hand on her hip, and gave him the best evil eye Sean had ever witnessed, even pausing before she spoke. "Then how is it he rode *my* horse? The one that was stolen from me?"

Stolen now?

The man was slack jawed. "I don't see how that can be true so that makes you a liar!" The man returned Tommy's querulous tone before facing Sean. "If you're bent on making trouble, the sheriff is in town today."

That would be best if Sean were home but this man sounded Norman. The Sheriff was definitely Norman. What are the chances he'd get justice? And what about Tommy? He didn't know all the details but he was not certain about her coming up before a sheriff.

He decided to change tactics. "Are ye threatening me?"

"Only if you give me trouble."

"Ye took my money. Ye told me to use the horse and bring her back and then ye gave me a stolen horse. The owner wants it back!"

The man glanced between the two of them, a frown as deep as the River Liffey between his eyes. "The lad's a liar. 'Tis not a stolen horse. That horse had been brought to me just the day before—"

"Ah, yer memory is returning then!" Sean crossed his arms.

The man heaved his chest with his sigh. "I remember the horse, not you! And it was not stolen. The man had just won her in a bet and needed her kept here until he returned from up north."

Sean glanced at Tommy. Her wide eyes were trained on the man as if he were a snake about to bite her.

"The man had won himself a bride as well."

Tommy turned a bright shade of red. She backed away slightly, suddenly unsure on her feet.

"He was to be wed?"

"Said he'd return for the horse with his bride." The man wiped his hands on the filthy cloth at his waist. "Do you have the horse?"

"Nae."

"You shouldn't be listening to tales." He turned his gaze on Tommy. "Unless he's the one the man won it off." The man chortled and Tommy's color deepened.

Sean took the opportunity to take Tommy's arm despite her initial struggle against him and turn her about, away from the other man. "I'm leaving on the morrow. You can have her then—unless I find a witness who backs the lad's story."

He wanted the whole story but he wouldn't shame her here in front of this man by demanding explanations. They made it out of the lean-to and kept moving. Anger lengthened his stride and she was winded as he pulled her along.

"What is amiss? Why are we running away?"

Sean wouldn't answer her. Not here. He needed a quiet place. He needed to get some answers. Before he realized where he was headed, they were up the hill and behind the village. The trees again giving them shelter from wary eyes.

He let go of her arm and began pacing. Strong emotions stirred inside. Emotions like anger. Like stupidity. Like regret.

"I'm not one to pry. Believe me that I would rather just walk away from this whole messy situation but I've a bit of a problem on my hands."

Tommy gave him a narrow gaze and pressed her lips tightly together. "What problem?"

"Ye!"

Her nostrils flared. "I am not a problem. I was trying to get my horse back."

"The horse that yer betrothed won in a game of chance from yer father?"

She gasped. A very girlish gasp. Her breasts heaving in her upset. Her cheeks reddened. Her eyes rounded. His breath stilled inside him. She was beautiful.

"Ye dunna ken the whole story," she said.

"I dunna want to ken the whole story. I dunna give a damn." Anguish flashed over her face. Sean felt a surprising burst of guilt across his chest but he pushed on." I have my own problems. I dunna need yers. I want to go home."

"I never asked for yer help! I only wanted my horse."

"It was my horse until I returned it. Then it could be yer horse again."

"It wasna his to give out."

"It appears ye're wrong!" Sean's raised voice surprised him. He was more heated than he would expect. All he had to do was walk away from her. Just head into town, go to his room, and wait for the boat on the morrow. Instead he stood here wanting to… punch someone in the face or something just as drastic. Damn it. He couldn't very well abandon her now.

~

Thomasina bit her lip to keep it from quivering. She would be damned to hell before she cried in front of this beef-witted oaf.

"I will just go take my horse. Be on my way. Ye can go home."

She glanced around. The area felt more exposed than it had earlier.

"Ye dunna have yer horse." Sean sounded almost reasonable.

Her suspicions piqued. "Yea, I do. She's tethered at the green."

"Nae. That is *my* horse. I must return her in order to get the knife back."

"Nae." Her knees threatened to give way. She was exhausted, like she hadn't slept for days. She just wanted to be home with her brother and safe from their father. "Ye canna do that."

He took a step closer. "It was not my knife to leave. I—I was irritated with one of my kinsman. I acted rashly."

"He will understand," she begged him.

"He will not! 'Tis of great value to him."

What was she to do? Return home? To her father? And just accept that old man as her husband? No! Life could not be this cruel. What past transgression was she paying for? She collapsed on the ground.

"Fine. Yea. Ye should go see to this knife. Go quick." She looked heavenward at the smattering of stars just appearing beyond the trees. "Although it may be too late. The blacksmith may be gone by now."

She glanced back at him. "But ye can always sleep in yer warm bed. In yer solitary room. Swive the lovely red-headed wench. Then ye can return my horse, get yer treasured knife back and be off, across the sea to... what? A wife is it? An important chieftain ye serve?"

She dropped her head into her hands, no longer needing the pretense of being a strong lad. She closed her eyes. It didn't matter. If she stayed here, her brother may come this way. He may not. He and his friends had been off stealing newborn ewes so they could come this way. Maybe. It had been a long time since their father provided for his family. He preferred to provide for himself. Strong liquor. A game of chance.

The gentle touch on her arm startled here. She straightened up. Sean kneeled beside her, smelling of horses and leather.

"I'm sorry. I will try to work this out for ye," he said. His eyes wide in the darkness.

"Nae. 'Tis not yer problem. I'm sorry I called Daisy. I should have let ye pass and hope to catch up with her... somewhere. I dinna mean to cause ye any problem."

She swiped at her cheek.

"Sure. Now ye look like a lad with that smear of dirt across yer face."

"Is that all I missed? A dirty face?" Her voice was quiet. She had little left to expend on talking. No warm bed for her. No nice fire. At least her stomach was full. "Thank ye for seeing to my food."

"Don't be sad, *Tommy*." He brushed at the dirt on her face. "Tell me yer real name."

"I am called Tommy."

His look of disbelief showed in the moonlight. "So now we tell each other more lies?"

"'Tis the truth! I am called Tommy." She rubbed at her nose. "My mother? She called me Thomasina."

"Ah, ye do look more like a Thomasina." He brushed her hair away from her face, his calloused fingers sweeping across her cheek. A shiver worked its way through her insides, settling down low.

Mesmerized, she watched him lick his finger and swipe at her cheek. Her mother would do just that and she'd be mad as the devil. His touch felt different... more intimate. He cupped her face with a gentle hand. "That's better. Do ye ken where we can find yer brother?"

She shook her head, overwhelmed with the impossibility of her situation. "Not for certain."

Taking his hand from her face, she looked into his eyes. "I will not be yer burden. I will return up the hill and wait for my brother like he told me to."

"When was that?"

She looked away. "Four or five days ago." A lie. "He'll be back any time. I will be fine."

"Who is it ye're marrying?"

A surge of repulsion that felt like she was about to throw up forced her to her feet. "Nae one. I am not marrying anyone."

He fell off his knees to land on his backside. His eyes wide with surprise. She offered her hand to help him up. Tipping his head to the side, he eyed her hand before searching her face. He touched his fingers to hers. Lightning flashed up her arm, making it difficult to catch her breath.

Sean entwined their fingers then tugged her down next to his lap. She felt tiny beside him, her knees bent beneath her. His face so close she could see the little lines around his eyes. He placed his arm across her chest, grabbing her far shoulder. Those arms strong enough to crush an enemy. He smiled. Then with a quick heave, she was flat across his lap. Her bottom raised in the air.

"Hey!" she said.

"Now how about an honest talk?" His tone laced with irritation. "And ye can try telling me the truth if ye even have a spot of truth anywhere in ye."

CHAPTER 6

Sean had expected her to struggle which was why he had her arm tucked between his body and hers, and her other arm held tight to her side. What he had not expected was to be so affected by her. Alarm bells were sending waves of regret—and overwhelming desire—coursing through him. Not one of his finest moments. If she ever settled down, she'd certainly find his arousal as upsetting as her anticipated punishment. He had no plans to actually slap her bottom, he just wanted honest answers. He found a threat worked best.

"So before I land my hand on yer arse since ye're so deserving—oof." Her elbow poked into his stomach, knocking the air out of him. He pulled her closer in to him and raised his knees to keep her lodged there. "—how about ye try telling me the truth for once and *then* I can be on my way."

"Ye whoreson! Who do ye think ye are? Let me go!" She continued her struggles.

Her tempting bottom wiggling from side to side was hard to ignore. He needed to disarm her and quickly. "What? Nae clearing of yer throat to sound like a lad?"

"Let me go." She pulled her knees in and managed to plow into his groin. The pain excruciating. He reacted with a hard slap to her bottom.

She stilled. He held his breath until the sharp pain lessened then yanked her legs out straight.

He adjusted her away from him to ease the pressure on his groin. She didn't need to know specifically what she had managed to do. "Try that again and I'll make ye sorry."

"I'll make *ye* sorry!" she hollered back at him.

He didn't hide the smile. She remained motionless across his lap. Her delightful bottom at his disposal but he refrained from touching her.

"I'm not an idiot. I ken when ye're lying to me and here I've done nothing but try to assist ye."

"Assist me? Was that when ye insulted me? Told me I was girly?"

"Ye are a girl!"

"And is that what ye wanted me to tell ye?" She rolled back so she could look him in the face. "Is that why ye teased me mercilessly?"

"Nae! I wanted ye to remember to act like a boy, damn it! Ye kept slipping up! How could I take ye to the village with everyone seeing ye for what ye are? They'd have been all over ye like ticks on a dog."

"Ye bastard!" She started kicking her legs with wild abandon. "Let me go. Let me go."

With one arm wrapped around her narrow waist, he stood, holding her like a sack of corn. Placing her away from him, he held each arm in a firm grip against her side. She hunched forward, breathing heavy from the exertion. And all he could think about was covering her mouth with his, of tasting her lips, her skin, of running his fingers through her tangled mane. He was near exploding with desire for her.

"Stop this! I deserve to ken the truth." Sean's voice sounded strained and he prayed she wouldn't realize why. "Thomasina!"

It was a beautiful name. It fit her perfectly.

Closing her mouth, Tommy looked to be getting herself under control. Her eyes on him, she shook as if overcome by his audacity. Mayhap he should have taken to paddling her as she so deserved but he feared he'd feel worse than she would. Beating a woman was not in his nature. That one spank had been an unexpected reaction to pain. Slapping her bottom was the farthest thing from what he wanted to do with it.

"Truth!" he groaned aloud. "Put me out of my misery."

She looked surprised at his outburst then took a shaky breath. "Yea! Ye deserve the truth."

"And do ye ken the truth?" Sean leveled his gaze. "I dunna need any more pretenses here. Not now."

Not when his body yearned to be betwixt her legs as he pounded into her, receiving his need, answering with her own passion. She had no idea. She would have no idea. He kept his gaze fixed on her face despite the heaving breasts and the sweat trickling down her neck into places he'd like to follow with his tongue.

"Can we sit?" she asked.

He feared she planned to bolt. "I canna release ye. I dunna trust ye not to run."

Incredulity poured out from her. "How can ye—"

"Ye've been lying to me since the moment I met ye. How can I suddenly trust ye?"

"Do ye want to ken or not?"

"Nae!" He'd prefer not to but his preference wasn't of much consequence now. He'd have preferred to not have met her dressed as a lad, stealing his horse out from under him, and all but scratching at herself to make the pretense believable. He'd prefer to have met her in the village, dressed in a gown that clung to all her womanly curves, plying him with a "come hither" look that promised much, and her hair soft around her shoulders where he could rub its silkiness against his cheek instead of shoved down her shirt as if it were something to be forgotten. He licked his lips. "Yea."

Her arms still in his grip, they settled onto the ground at the same time, facing each other.

She nodded, her breath growing steadier. "Yea. I am sorry to have had to lie to ye."

"Ye dunna ken anything about me. How do ye ken ye had to lie to me?"

"I canna trust anyone."

"Yea. Ye could only take my horse."

"Oh! Not fair!"

"But the truth! And that is what we're working on here. Are we not?"

She sighed. "Yea. The truth."

The silence grew and he watched the emotions flit across her face. If she knew how easily he could read her... "Dunna think half-truths will work. I ken when ye're lying."

"*Hmph!* About a week ago, my father told me my betrothed would be coming to wed me that afternoon."

"Ye *were* betrothed then?" A heaviness settled in his chest. She was spoken for.

"Nae! And ye canna be interrupting!"

Sean tipped his head. She was being annoying on purpose. He gripped her chin to tip it up toward him. He glanced at her lips. A strong impulse to kiss her washed over him. He glanced into her eyes instead, narrowing them for effect. "I willna be put off. I'm staying here until I get the truth from ye. All of it."

"I was not betrothed! So," she stressed the last word.

Sean released her chin and rolled his eyes but said nothing. His fingers fidgeted along her wrist, her pulse racing beneath his fingers.

"I asked him when this had all transpired," she said.

He nodded encouragement, wishing she'd hurry up with her explanation. Staying this close made it difficult to think. The sudden urge to bring her wrist to his nose was overwhelming. Another trickle dripped beneath her shirt.

"Ye've bound yer breasts." It sounded like an accusation. Perhaps it was. His body tensed. The knife at his side could easily slice through the binding, releasing those glorious orbs. He glanced at her chest.

"How do ye—" she said.

He held his breath and released the grip he'd taken on his dagger. When he finally looked her in the face, her eyes were wide as if in sudden clarity. All that was missing was her *Ah-hah!*

"Ye're sweating a lot," he said.

The look was gone and she nodded. "Yea. The extra material is very hot."

He swallowed hard and pressed his tongue against the roof of his mouth. He needed to stop speaking.

She finally continued. "He told me he was in a bit of trouble and wedding me to the man he owed money would see to both his problems." She looked away, as if no longer able to meet his eyes. "Apparently having to find me a husband—" Her voice broke. "—was a problem to the man. I had nae idea."

Unfeeling bastard.

"I think he speaks of his own shortcomings. Nothing to do with ye."

She nibbled at her lip, shaking her head in a sad, defeated sort of way. "I just could not let the devil spawn marry me off like that." Thomasina turned to him suddenly. "He waited until my brother had left before telling me. Do ye think that was a coincidence? Oh nae! My brother would have put a stop to such ideas. My father drinks and—"

Her lips parted, her eyes rounded and she had one of those oh-no-I've-said-too-much expressions.

Sean released her arm, his hand caressing up and down, attempting to comfort. He tried to ignore the tingling shooting up his arm. "Dunna fash yerself."

His words reeked with desperation. He needed to stop talking.

She pierced him with her look. "Do ye understand what I'm saying?"

Sean let his hand fall away then sat back, a discreet distance from her, and took a slow, steady breath. He had to answer her. "My father drank himself into an early grave after my mother died. I was just ten."

Her gaze softened. "My brother would never have allowed him to marry me off to pay a debt. I went to take my horse in search of Niall but Daisy was gone. My father had given her to the man as well. He said he knew I'd want to be wherever my horse was."

Sean nodded again, a slow controlled movement.

"I was beside myself. I went to the cave my brother kept the animals in that he sto—acquired and found a few ewes penned. I cried myself to sleep and woke up to find three new lambs but nae sign of my brother or his raiding friends."

"So he does not even know what yer father has done?"

She shook her head, her forehead lined with worry.

"And will we find him here?"

She shook her head.

So how would he get distance from her? He couldn't continue to be near her and keep his hands off. She was far too enticing even dressed as a lad. "Where can we find yer brother?"

Her expression closed down. She'd heard the emotion in his voice. No doubt she assumed the worst.

"I'm sorry—" he said.

She looked away. "—I ken a few of the spots he goes but they were not there. Nae sign of them. That's when I saw ye on Daisy."

"Let me—"

"—I'm sorry for getting ye involved." She pulled her knees up to her chest and rested her chin there, still avoiding looking right at him. "All I can ask is that ye leave me to my own trouble. I'll work it out on my own. In my own way."

She wouldn't let him explain how he felt. What would he say? That he lusted after her? That he'd be slaking himself on her if given the opportunity. He would not tell her that.

"Well," Sean stood and offered his hand. She didn't take it. "I'm willing to look after ye and find yer brother."

"What?" She finally faced him. "Nae!"

"I'm not about to leave ye unprotected, lass." Sean's gut tightened. Why he stepped right into the hornet's nest was beyond him. "'Tis no problem despite what ye may think ye ken. We will locate yer brother."

It was indeed a problem but Sean would not abandon her. She had guts. He admired that. Her father was a whoreson but her brother sounded decent. He'd track him down and then be on his way.

"What is yer brother's name? Niall?"

"Yea."

"Then we'll find Niall."

Besides she'd only get into more trouble on her own. Dark circles were etched under her eyes. Tears had left tracks down her dirty cheeks. Her hair was a rat's nest. If he knew women at all, this lass would be appreciating a bath right now.

"Enough talk. I have the room."

Thoughts of her in the bed with him were a bit much and he walked on ahead of her. Torn between walking behind her so no one else noticed the shapely arse of the young lad and walking ahead to work off some...

energy, Sean led the way until near the opened wooden door of the establishment. The sounds inside were raucous and spilled out into the street.

"I canna go in there! That woman. She knows."

"Ye can sneak in the back." Sean winked at her.

Sean went around the building and found it as he expected, empty. No one saw to the cooking fire. Eating had shifted to drinking. That and fornication.

Thomasina followed at a distance. In the dim light cast by the moon, he waved his arm to draw her forward. He pulled her close to be certain she heard him. A mistake.

The top of her head came just to his chest. She leaned in to peer through the dimly lit room, touching him. She smelled delicious despite her unwashed state. He took her elbow making to steady her but he knew it was just to feel her beneath his fingers. He could easily span her narrow waist with both hands. The urge to pull her against him for a kiss increased with her nearness.

Sean forced his mind to focus. "See the stairs to the left?"

The steps were tucked into the far corner of the building.

"Yea."

"When they're not looking this way, cross over to the stairs. The room is right at the top."

"Ye've been here before?"

The memory of the dark-haired woman faded now. She'd been insistent and Tadhg had encouraged Sean to see to his needs so she'd all but dragged him upstairs. Fighting the woman off had been a first for him. When Sean came down, he told Tadhg he'd declined her offer and wanted to wait to be wed to Brighit before slaking himself. Tadhg laughed as if he'd proposed some absurd possibility. If he could see him now all but panting for this lass dressed like a lad, he'd be doubled over with laughter.

"Aye. I came with others and we… well I avoided… yea, I've been here before."

~

Thomasina's heart raced at the very idea of trying to cross the room without being seen. She closed her eyes and took a deep breath. There was no other choice. Sean tried to help her and she had to trust him. She opened her eyes and looked up at him. His eyes were, again, assessing her. Perhaps trying to determine what she really looked like without a lad's disguise.

His eyes pierced hers. Her breath hitched. The look of longing was there then quickly gone. Had she imagined it? He smiled. An innocent smile. A you're-safe-with-me smile. So why was the intensity of his gaze making her feel lightheaded? Why was she wishing she were properly attired as a woman to see if that look of longing would return?

"Ye can wait here," Sean said. "I'll go in through the front and when they're not looking, ye can go in."

She nodded.

An owl hooted nearby. The clouds drifted in front of the moon. The woods a few feet from the building darkened behind them. Sean went around to the front. Standing back, hidden in the trees, she watched him as he ducked to come in through the door.

The owner welcomed him back but looked a bit disappointed. Sean looked huge standing in the entrance to the room. Her stomach fluttered. All the men around him were smaller, shorter, and not nearly as handsome. His long, blond hair and the darker shade of his beard gave him a savage look.

The redhead came forward, placing her hand flat against Sean's broad chest. She tucked herself in close. Thomasina clenched her jaw. Sean took a step back, putting the wench away from him. The owner moved quickly through the crowd of men and away from them, his eyes darting about the room. He disappeared up the stairs.

The woman pushed against Sean with her body, flattening her humongous breasts against him when he tried to go past. He dipped toward her head, his mouth close to her ear, to say something to her. Pain shot through Thomasina's jaw.

The owner came back down and looked toward the redhead who kept Sean distracted. Thomasina wondered if Sean realized what was happening. It seemed an obvious ploy. With an eye on Sean, the owner motioned behind to someone up the stairs. A tall man in a hooded cloak followed behind. He refused to be hurried. With a jutting chin and his nose in the air, he followed the nervous man. When she realized they were heading toward her, Thomasina jerked back into the trees.

"My apologies, my lord. I didn't expect the warrior back tonight." The owner spoke in hushed tones. "Does he upset any plans?"

"No. We'll be meeting anon." The hooded man said more but Thomasina didn't catch it as they walked the length of the building toward the road.

The two men stopped just short of the front corner of the inn. Facing each other, their voices now carried to her.

"I hope you and Lady Abigail found the accommodations—"

"Enough!" The man's commanding tone silenced the innkeeper. "Keep to the plan."

"Yes, my lord."

"Be certain to have the irons hot for our return. We'll see these usurpers get what they deserve."

The hooded man pulled his cloak tight around his face and stepped into the street, heading off to the right.

A woman with long, black hair came down the stairs at the same time, stopping just within the entryway. She tilted her head back and glanced around the room. She had full, red lips and a fair complexion that complemented her dark her. She was beautiful. She scurried toward Thomasina, glanced both ways once outside, then moved along the path in the opposite direction of the men before veering into the woods. The sweet aroma of flowers drifted to Thomasina and lingered after she'd passed.

The owner came through the front door. He smoothed his hair, planted a broad smile on his face, then walked toward Sean. He directed Sean to the stairs, said something, then laughed. The redhead went off toward the men at the table. Sean went up the stairs without glancing toward Thomasina.

Her breathing sped up. She swallowed against her fear and came out of the protective trees to approach the building. The men in the room were well into their cups. She recognized the signs. Loud voices and random bursts of laughter. Her skin crawled. Certainly they would not notice a lad coming through the back door. Sean's words came back to her about their needs and how even a lad that looked like a girl would suffice. Bile rose in her throat.

She watched the goings-on from just outside the door. Some type of contest with three men seated and the rest circling them. The redhead made her presence known by squeezing herself between the men standing around. An occasional call for more mead was the only time any of them looked up from the action. The owner waited just inside to Thomasina's right, where the libations were kept behind the trestle table.

"Yes. Yes. I'm coming." The owner moved toward the circle of men.

Thomasina took a deep breath and held it. She made her way toward the stairs which suddenly seemed a great distance away.

"Hey. Stop!" It was a man's angry voice.

She froze. Laughter erupted behind her. She swallowed down the saliva flooding her mouth and turned to face the man. No one looked her way.

"You whoring Norman! What do you think? You can cheat us?"

"Don't slander me so! I'm no Norman."

Clearing the entrance to the stairs, she ducked inside and fell against the wall. She panted like she'd run a great race.

"Up here!" Sean stood at the top stair. An opening behind allowed light to reveal a small area where stores were kept. Sacks were stacked four high beside him.

She climbed the steps two at a time and collapsed on the floor in the tiny room.

He reached down to take her elbow and help her up. "Easy, lass. Ye've made it. Ye're safe."

She couldn't speak. Who did she think she was going off on her own to get her brother? She didn't have courage. She was a milksop! Tears rimmed her eyes and the room blurred.

His blue eyes widened with concern. "Easy now. Ye're shaking!"

"I'm sorry. I'm—"

Loud voices carried up the stairs as if someone had moved much closer. Sean shifted to quickly close the rough-hewn door. He leaned his forehead against it and listened. Satisfied, he turned toward her with a smile.

"Hell of a gathering going on down there." His smile dropped. He rubbed the back of his neck.

The room was barely big enough for a normal sized man to stand in. Sean hunched forward as he moved to the far side where the thatched ceiling pitched even lower. He turned toward her, the water skin she recognized from last night in his hand.

Thomasina held up her hand to ward him off when he came toward her. The stuff tasted like horse piss. "Nae! I dunna want any."

He pressed her hand down, a slight smile on his lips. "Just a bit. Ye're quaking like a leaf."

Thomasina covered her mouth. "I nearly threw up downstairs."

Sean moved closer, rubbing her back with small circles. The soothing motion abruptly shifted to her shoulders. "This is different. It goes down easy."

Shaking gripped her and she couldn't stop it. Her teeth chattered. She needed something so she accepted the heavy skin. She hoped her expression showed her disbelief at being able to keep it down.

Holding the skin with two hands, she tipped it toward her mouth and dribbled a few drops on her waiting tongue. Sean's eyes were dark as he watched her, his expression intent. Apparently it was very important that she accept this. It wasn't as bad as the other drink. She put the opening to her mouth, closed her eyes, and squeezed some of the liquid into her mouth. It felt warm—very warm—but didn't burn like the other. She swallowed then drank some more. She imagined the liquid forming a little relaxing puddle in her stomach. She took a deep, slow breath then blew it out. Her shaking eased. She'd made it.

When she opened her eyes, Sean's gaze had dropped to her hips. The fluttering began again. His eyes made a slow sweep of her from her trews up to her face. His lips parted.

She offered a small smile, no longer certain how to react. "Are ye afeared I'll drink all of yer precious mead?"

"Yea." His gaze held hers. "Something like that."

"This is much better than the other." She closed her eyes, relieved to shut out the confusing messages, and took another sip.

His fingers caressing her cheek startled her. She opened her eyes to find him standing very close.

"I'm glad 'tis to yer liking." His voice was low. He wrapped one hand around her, flattening ever so gently against the small of her back. He moved his face in closer. "Let me taste it."

Her breath caught. Her eyes closed. The touch of his lips sent a jolt right to her core. His mouth moved over hers. Searching. Insistent. A thoroughly enjoyable feeling. She leaned in closer. The slightest pressure and her lips parted, allowing the invasion of his warm, probing tongue. He groaned against her. She silently agreed.

She moved her tongue with his and he pulled her close against his length. His strong arms wrapped around her. Safe. Arousing. Her body relaxed against him. He groaned a second time, just lifting his lips.

"Mo mhíle stór," Sean spoke on a breath then his lips were on hers again.

His kisses grew more demanding. Heat swirled low in her stomach. He wanted something. She wanted him to have it. Whatever it was. His hand drifted lower down her back to cup her bottom, pulling her up against him and an unyielding stiffness. The swirling shifted lower. Heat poured off him and she basked in it. She moaned her pleasure. She wanted more. His arms fell away and he stepped back in one motion as if she'd burned him.

Disappointment washed over her like a wave and she stumbled to gain her footing. Her labored breathing the only sound. The sudden loss of his body was acute.

Her chest rose with each breath. "What is amiss?"

Sean pushed stray hairs away from his face with both hands. His eyes wide with incredulity. "Ye! What are ye doing? Dunna let a man touch ye like that!"

"I want ye to touch me like that."

Sean made a strangled sound in his throat and turned away. His shoulders rose and fell and he paced the small area. He finally stopped several feet away. "Nae. Ye dunna want me to."

"I like the way ye touch me."

"And dunna say that either."

A rock seemed to drop into the pit of her stomach. Her father had been right. Whatever this was that was happening had something to do with her being a problem to wed. Where there had been warmth and longing, she now felt loss and pain.

She crossed the few steps to the door and stopped. It was not safe for her to go back down there but she had trouble remembering why. It must be the drink but she knew going downstairs was worse than staying here. She faced Sean then slid down the door to sit in front of it.

"I'll sleep here."

Sean's expression softened. "Nae. NAE! Ye'll not. Ye'll sleep here." He indicated the pallet on the raised platform beside him. "I'll sleep on the floor. Ye sleep here and there will be nae more discussion."

Thomasina licked her lips and looked about for the skin. She didn't remember him taking it out of her hands. She did remember the way his hands felt grasping her bottom, pulling her against him. The heat still there between her legs. She searched him to see if she could discern the hardness. She could.

Sean fisted the skin at his side. As if reading her mind, he took a long draw then closed it tight. His breathing still shallow. She stood and walked to the pallet. It was filthy and covered with horse hair and fleas.

Glancing toward Sean whose gaze remained on her, she offered a sly smile. "Wonder what's happened here."

"And do ye ken, my worldly lass?"

"Nae. I dunna." She pointed to his groin. "I think it has to do with the condition ye're experiencing with yer prick."

"And ye'd be right."

"I saw a man and a woman sneak down these stairs when the redhead was… enticing ye."

"I wasna enticed."

"Are ye certain? Ye looked quite enticed earlier."

To be honest, he looked like he would have enjoyed jumping on her right then and there and… sticking her with that prick. Pain spread through her chest.

She'd heard a little of what happened between a man and a woman but not much. She was too young when her mother had died and there was no one else to tell her. Her father said little about anything. He preferred the drink to her company.

"Ye can go to her if ye want." A sob rose in her throat. She swallowed it down. "I can stay here without ye."

When he'd held her close to his body there had been a promise of something wonderful.

"Get to sleep," Sean said. He turned away from her and removed his sword, placing it on the little bench in the corner. He pulled his leine over his head.

She nearly gasped at the wide expanse of his back. The muscles rippled with the movement as he placed the shirt on the bench as well. The heat intensified between her legs. A longing to touch him made her palms itch. She gripped her hands together and exhaled. She crawled onto the bed and gave him her back.

He had stopped whatever was about to happen. She didn't understand why but watching him was not helping her settle down. Was there something about her that was an aversion to men? Mayhap her father was right. Mayhap she should return and let him marry her off. That man seemed interested. At least then her father's debt would be paid and she'd be doing something beneficial with herself.

CHAPTER 7

$\mathcal{A}$ high-pitched screech jerked Sean awake. He stood, sword in hand, before his eyes were opened all the way. A woman screamed again. He remembered where he was and glanced toward the pallet. It was empty. His heart leapt into his throat.

Sean yanked open the door. Laughing and loud talking drifted to him. Men up to no good. He walked soundlessly down the stairs, pausing to secure his sword and tuck the dagger from his boot into his belt, wishing he'd thought to don his leine.

Stopping a few steps from the bottom, he peered around the opening. The back door stood ajar. The red glow of the fire gave off little light. The owner no longer visible. Helmets, leather, and weapons were dropped by the front door as if men had entered in a hurry. Norman soldiers. There had been no soldiers earlier. The men that had been there were gone. Thomasina was not there either.

The red-headed wench was bent over the trestle table, her naked buttocks facing him. A tall, thin man kicked her feet wider and flattened her against the wooden surface before blocking Sean's view.

"Come on now, ye Saxon bitch." He yanked down his trews, his filthy, bare arse exposed. "One for me now."

The men around them laughed. He covered her and the men cheered him on. There was a movement outside. As if in a dream, the scene unfolded before Sean. Nell screeched again. Thomasina came through the door and froze, her eyes locked on the man with Nell. Her mouth dropped open.

"Stop!" Her words held the ring of authority but sounded distinctly feminine.

The men turned toward her. Their surprise visible in the frowns and raised eyebrows, and they quickly sized her up. An eerie assortment of grunts, grumbles, and what he'd swear were groans of appreciation filled Sean's ears. Dagger in one hand, sword in the other, he leapt into the room with a thud.

The men's attention quickly diverted to him. Their eyes widened with surprise and fear. One little man with a nasty grin that had shifted toward Thomasina halted and faced him.

"I believe the lad said to stop." Sean's booming voice filled the small space.

The soldiers glanced around as if to ask what they were supposed to do. Their eyes came to rest on one man. A blotchy-faced, chicken-chest of a man sitting off to the side, watching. His greasy, brown hair streaked with gray pulled back from his face. Their leader.

"Step away from the woman," Sean ordered.

The man stepped away with slow movements as if afraid he might be run through before he complied. His stiffened cock wagged in front of him before he thought to pull his trews up.

Sean walked further into the room. He signaled with his head for Thomasina to get up the stairs. She listened without comment.

"The woman is for hire." Sean lowered his weapons just slightly. A signal that if they wanted to be reasonable, he was willing. "Why force her?"

The leader stood, adjusted himself, and walked toward Sean. His head only came up to Sean's shoulder which he grasped before he spoke. "My friend, the problem is… we don't want to pay."

Sean glanced at Nell who righted her clothing. She spat at the man who had been about to impale her. He moved to slap her but Sean's sword was quicker when he placed it between them and shook his head. The man glanced toward their leader who gave a barely discernible nod of his head before backing down.

"Men need their sport."

"She does not have an aversion to the sport. She's merely trying to feed herself," Sean said.

The leader dropped his hand and nodded thoughtfully. "But these are good Norman soldiers. They're keeping the countryside free from… rabble."

"Ye're taking her wares."

Their leader narrowed his eyes at this. His steely gaze seemed to be measuring Sean's willingness to fight over this woman. Sean focused his attention on the man. His willingness to fight was without question.

"So you believe each man here should pay to fuck her?"

"Otherwise it would be stealing. Ye ken?"

Their leader's lips pressed into a stiffened line as if hiding his amusement. He raised his eyebrows in a questioning expression. "Where are you from?"

The soldiers tensed toward Sean as if waiting to hear his answer.

Sean lifted the tip of his blade just a hair. "I am from the west."

Nervous glances toward their gear left by the door heightened Sean's readiness for battle. His size alone usually kept men at a distance. He had no problem taking them on either.

"Across the sea!" Their leader smirked at him then glanced at his men. "Ye ken?"

They laughed as if on cue.

"You're a dumb farmer?" The man at Sean's left shifted his feet after he'd asked the question. His face disfigured and reddened, possibly from boiling water or tar. A battle-seasoned soldier.

"You've the right of it, Will," the leader said.

Sean stood straighter. He looked down on the man. His expression tight. "Dumb? Nae."

The disfigured man sneered, his lips and chin the only area unmarred, and moved in closer. "What are you then?"

"A warrior."

All sound stopped in the room. No one dared to breathe. There were only seven of them. He'd won in more uneven matches than this. That's when he'd been the only one he needed to think about. Sean wished Thomasina had a means of escape from the area he'd relegated her to. Protecting her from these men was paramount.

"So are yer men willing to pay for their… satisfaction?" Sean questioned.

"I don't want their blood money." Nell let loose her outrage at their treatment. "They can just leave. Go!" She directed them to the door with a sweep of her hand. "Go!"

Sean had hoped to defuse the situation but lusty men coming from battle were not to be provoked. Her anger at them would cause resentment. A lesson apparently lost on the wench.

"Mayhap a drink for ye."

Sean froze. He swallowed hard and had to stop his jaw from dropping at the sound of Thomasina's voice from behind him.

"Can I get that for ye?" she asked.

The soldiers' eyes narrowed with suspicion. The leader tipped his head as if assessing this newest development. He watched her as she crossed in front of them, running his thumb along his bottom lip. Sean's breath caught at the sight of her rounded bottom. Mayhap he should have mentioned that little oversight of her costume instead of making it his mission to block anyone else's perusal.

She stretched across the trestle where Nell had just been held down against her will and offered a good view to all the soldiers. A collective groan of appreciation then sideways glances between a few of the men. Turning to face them with two jugs now in hand, she smiled.

The leader closed the distance to her in two steps, accepting the jug with a slight bow before placing it on the table.

"Aye. I'll take that." He snaked his arm around Thomasina's back and turned her to face front. He held her up against him. His arm tight around her, just under her breasts which were thankfully bound. A knife glistened in his other hand, close to her neck. "And anything else I like."

Sean didn't move. He didn't breathe. He didn't dare react at all.

The men's sighs of relief quickly changed to hoots and hollers of triumph. One man slapped Nell's arse.

"You like this one don't you, Warrior?" The leader's smile reached his eyes this time, no doubt convinced he now had the upper hand.

Sean had hoped the men had missed his earlier interchange with Thomasina. If she'd stayed above, it wouldn't have mattered if they hadn't.

"Be at ease, men," the leader announced in a loud voice. "There's no worry here." Thomasina gasped, the blade against her skin. "He won't be stopping you from your fun now."

The man who had been about to mount Nell jerked her close and threw her back on the table. He yanked her skirts up, spread her legs, and freed his ready cock.

They all nodded with appreciation, moving in close, ready to take their turn. Others moved about the room helping themselves to libations as if Sean were no longer present. Occasional nervous glances were the only sign that he still held their attention. His chest heaved in one low breath. He kept his eyes locked on Thomasina's which were wide with fear. He pressed his lips together and his nostrils flared.

"Holding a lad hostage does not seem very soldier-like," Sean said.

"No? I assure you 'tis very soldier-like in our army." The leader guffawed and the others joined in. He turned Thomasina's head, forcing her face toward him. "Bet you have a tight little arse." He glanced at Sean without turning toward him. "Does he? Is that why you keep him to yourself?"

When his hand began its descent toward Thomasina's backside, Sean pitched himself forward, his sword pointed straight out in front. In the blink of an eye, he speared the man through the chest. The dagger dropped harmlessly to the floor. Sean withdrew the sword as the body dropped to the ground. He shoved Thomasina behind him when he turned around to face the others. His sword at the ready before any of them even realized their leader was dead.

"Any other takers?" Sean asked.

Nell elbowed the man who was just positioning himself and rounded on him. She kicked him in the groin and he dropped to the floor with a hiss of pain. The scarred man took a step toward her.

"Enough!"

A large sound—a Saxon war cry—erupted outside. Sean's blood surged in response to the primal sound. The grip on his sword tightened. The front door flew open, banging against the wall with the impetus. The soldiers' eyes locked on to the armed men pouring into the room. The *rabble*. Armed with blades, axes, daggers, clubs, and a burning desire to rid themselves of the Normans' abuses.

The soldiers stilled. Any chance to get their weapons blocked by the oncoming men. With no way to protect themselves, this would be a slaughter. Sean raised his sword, unsure which side he was on. Battle lust heightening his awareness. The woman behind him trembled uncontrollably. He could smell her fear.

Against the six unarmed Normans, the mob advanced, attacking without mercy. Slashing. Stabbing. Slicing. All staying clear of Sean.

Sean recognized Ivan, his beady, little eyes glistening with excitement where he watched from the doorway beside a much taller, hooded man. Blood squirted from the man closest to Nell as he dropped. The bald man from earlier had sliced the man's throat, nearly decapitating him. The wench screamed in horror then worked her way through the malaise to the door, keeping her gown out of the blood that quickly pooled along the hard, dirt floor.

Thomasina shifted closer to Sean. The movement kept Sean's focus on protecting her. He took her hand and made his way toward the front, against the tide of incoming men who shoved past him. They were intent on the Normans alone and had no interest in him. Sean and Thomasina were able to leave the room unmolested.

Outside, the death throes of the men could be heard mingling with the eerie, night sounds of wild beasts howling as if in sympathy. Sean and Thomasina ran to the grazing area where her horse was. He leapt onto Roana then reached his arm around Thomasina's small middle to pull her in front of him. He cradled her against his chest. She was ice cold. A rein on either side, he turned the animal back toward the road.

A small, dark figure stood blocking their path. Ivan. "You not going to help us purge the land of these Normans?"

"I have no fight with the Normans."

"They've killed and raped and if they can do it here, it won't be long before they make it over the sea."

Sean had seen the proof of what he said. He needed to get Thomasina away. "Ye prefer chaos then? Slaughter like this?"

Ivan stepped closer. He glanced between Sean and Thomasina. "The end is the same. Taking back the land."

"Take it back from the Normans? For who? The Danes?"

Ivan laughed. "The Danes had their chance. No. Not the Danes. The Godwins."

The animal sidestepped away from Ivan.

Sean had heard there were no Godwins that survived the battle when the Normans invaded. "I think ye'd be hard pressed to find a Godwin to crown."

Ivan nodded. A slow, calculated nod as if he were assessing a game he planned to win. "I wouldn't be so quick to think that. Will you fight with us then?"

"Not like this." Sean tipped his head toward the inn where the sounds of the dead and dying could still be heard. He pulled the reins to go around the little man. Ivan stood fast then stepped away and allowed them to pass.

Sean urged the animal into a gallop and the darkness. The mayhem and massacre left far behind.

Thomasina woke up slowly, the sandy ground beneath her prickling at her skin, working into her trews and bindings. She itched all over.

"*Argh.*" She moaned in irritation before she opened her eyes.

Above her was the high, jagged ceiling that looked very much like the one in the cave her brother had left the ewes in.

Baaaa.

Thomasina jumped to her feet and looked around. The deer skin brat fell away from her to drop onto the floor. The same cave. The very one she had waited for her brother in. She glanced around. Where was Sean? Had he left her here and gone off to his life in Eire? A heaviness overwhelmed her. She dropped to the ground, rolling into a ball and covering herself again. Just as well. She had run out of options. Her only choice was to return to her father and be married off according to his wishes.

With her hands tucked under her head like a pillow, she closed her eyes to dream. Her father couldn't touch those. He could order her where to go, what to do, who to marry, but not what to dream.

It was a beautiful loch nestled against a towering hill with heather and thistle. The place of her childhood when her mother still lived. The scent of lavender and honeysuckle filling the air and wild berries growing all around. She and Daisy could walk along the stream, stripping down to nothing if she wanted to take a swim. Nobody would care. She would be alone.

A tightening in her belly. Maybe not alone. She didn't want to be alone. Maybe Sean would be there. With his broad chest and chiseled stomach. Hard as a rock. His arms safely around her. Anyone that came to insult her or hurt her would have to face him. He wouldn't back down. He would stand up to anyone who would harm her.

They would work together to care for the livestock, work the land, and raise their many wee ones. And at night... he would hold her close. She could hear his heart beating. And she could touch him. She could run her fingers from neck to waist. No. She would stroke him from the firm tanned column of his neck, down his broad chest, over his rippled belly, dipping down to grasp his fine, hard prick. That fluttering was there again. Low, down between her legs.

"What are ye about?"

Thomasina lurched to sitting up, her mouth hanging open, feeling as if she'd been caught eating the last hunk of bread.

"What? Oh. Nothing."

Sean crossed in front of her, his steps heavy as if he were tired. "Ye were making noise."

Her face heated. She hadn't realized. "I thought I was alone."

He glanced toward her, a deep frown creasing his handsome face. Placing two large fish on the rock, he came to stand in front of her. He crossed his arms in such a way that she knew he was angry. She waited.

"Alone?" he finally asked.

Her breath caught. He was a fine-looking man. Awareness heightened her senses. It was as if having been in his arms, his body now called out to her, drawing her to him. She was safe in his arms. She would miss him when he left. She followed the dark line of hair down his belly that disappeared into his trews. She licked her parched lips.

"Are ye without a leine now?"

He didn't budge. No acknowledgement that he'd heard her say anything. "Alone? Ye thought I had abandoned ye here?"

She shrugged. It didn't matter what she thought. It didn't matter what she felt. It didn't matter what she said. "How long have I been asleep?"

"Through the night and now most of the day."

"How did ye find this place?"

"The loud sound of bleating sheep helped me locate the spot." He tipped his head toward the pen. "There's only five. How many did ye say there were?"

She glanced toward the animals. They'd grown. Dirty, little bodies with dark faces. Snared and stuck with no way out. Sadness swamped her only to be replaced by nothingness. "I dunna remember."

Sean turned away in a display of his impatience. "Back to that are we?"

"And what would *that* be?"

"Prevarication."

Exasperation tightened her gut. Maybe not quite nothingness. She stood, her feet in a wide stance. "I said I dunna remember. Quite a lot has happened since then."

Images of squirting blood, skin sliced open, limbs being separated from their bodies all flashed through her mind. And the sounds. Men crying out in agony. She dropped again to the floor feeling too weak to stand.

Sean was right there, kneeling beside her. His hand caressed her back with a light touch. "I ken ye've been through a lot. Such things are a trial even to a seasoned warrior."

She searched his face. "I am afraid."

He settled on the ground and gathered her in his arms, her head against his solid chest. The heat poured off him.

The sound of his heart beating steadily was like a balm, a reassurance that they were alive. He was alive. She rubbed her face against him, snuggling closer. He tightened his hold on her.

"Wheesht now, lassie." He bent his head toward her, his lips close to her ear. She felt the warmth of his breath. A shiver traveled down her spine. "'Tis over. 'Tis done with."

She wrapped her arm around his torso, wanting him closer still.

"Wheesht."

"What goes on here?"

Thomasina's eyes flew open. Fear leaped to life within her, closing off her lungs. She shoved off the strong chest of the man to stand and face her worst nightmare. Her father.

"What are ye doing, girl? Have ye given up the only thing of value ye have to this ruffian?"

Sean stood as well, more slowly. She sensed the tension in him at the insult. Her eyes bore into the disheveled man before her. His eyes bloodshot. Jowls wagging with his angry words. Her sire. She didn't speak. She couldn't speak.

"Did ye hear me? Are ye going to leave me standing here without an answer?" He put his fisted hands to his hips and glanced around the cave. "Yer brother here as well?"

He didn't appear drunk but it had been a very long time since she'd seen him sober. Sean stood beside her.

Her father took a step closer, bending his head back to look up at Sean. "And who to hell are ye? And what are ye doing with yer arms about my only, precious daughter?" His lips curled into a menacing scowl. "Or did ye not realize she was a lass?"

"I realized she was a lass." Sean's voice steady. A stern visage.

Her father faced her, his eyes surveying her clothing as if she were covered in manure. "What were ye thinking? I've nothing else to give the man but yer virginity."

She swallowed hard. "The man? The one ye *sold* me to?"

"Who to hell else would want ye?" Without warning, he yanked her arm and pulled her away from Sean. He made as if to grab her back but her father's eyes widened in warning. "Dunna be getting involved with something that is none of yer concern."

Sean relaxed his stance. Like a strong, solid oak tree. Unmovable.

Her father's face close to hers, she could smell his foul breath. "Answer me. Have ye been spreading yer legs for this one?"

A hysterical laugh echoed in her head. She would not let it out. One long breath steadied her nerves. Her arm hurt from the tight grasp her father had of her. He shook her.

"Do ye hear me? Ye've no value at all without yer virginity. Are ye going to tell me what I need to know? Are ye this man's whore now?" His voice rasped in his anger. "Or are ye still innocent?"

"I have never been innocent with ye as my father."

The slap was hard against the side of her head. It sent her to the ground. Her ear rang, disorienting her, but she was aware of Sean bending toward her.

"Stand back now." Her father was giving the orders. "Unless ye've wed her—and I dunna see why ye would if she's giving it away—she's my responsibility and I'll see to her as I see fit."

Sean moved away, his feet shifting behind her.

"She is not giving it away." Sean's voice sounded reasonable, even keeled, but she recognized the barely held emotions filling his words. He was ready to erupt. She shook her head to clear it and came to stand beside her father. He was a bastard and she didn't want Sean to have to deal with him.

"He has not touched me."

The words squeezed her heart. She lied. He had touched her. Deeply. He had reached down inside and offered her acceptance of who she was. Dressed as a lad or not. It didn't matter to him. She didn't have to explain. He made her want something more than the constant ridicule and criticism that was her life.

"Then get on yer horse. Now." Her father's tone was final. "Yer betrothed is waiting on ye unless he's lost all interest."

Thomasina walked toward the opening to the cave. Her father followed behind and spoke over his shoulder at Sean.

"Dunna be giving me any trouble." Her father's ominous words carried to her. "Ye dunna want to ken what I can have done to the likes of ye."

"The likes of me?" Sean's voice was tight. He followed them. "And what likes would that be?"

"One hoping to get between Tommy's legs then leaving her behind."

"Ye dunna even ken me. How do ye ken I'd be leaving her?"

Her father halted and turned toward Sean. Thomasina stopped as well. Her feet refused to move.

"Why would ye stay?"

She didn't dare breathe. Her father must hate her.

"She's a bonny lass. I find her much to my liking."

"So what are ye offering me for her?"

Her breath caught in her chest. She couldn't get it out. The bastard. How could her mother have ever loved this man? No wonder she died so young.

"I hear ye found yerself owing the man? Her betrothed?" Sean's voice was warmer now as if they were just discussing the weather. A quick glance showed her he appeared relaxed. But then he crossed his arms in that we'll-just-see-about-that pose. "Tell me what the other man offered."

Her stomach dropped. They were discussing her worth? No. Not Sean. Father rubbed the unkempt gray beard at his chin in his pretense at thoughtfulness. "Well, well. Maybe I need to reconsider my options. Have ye anything of value?"

Sean smiled at him. The kind of smile that isn't sincere. The kind of smile that doesn't reach your eyes. The kind of smile that says you've outwitted someone. Sean had no idea how wrong he was. God help him.

CHAPTER 8

Sean's heart was in his throat. This man was the cruelest bastard he'd ever met. He all but screamed Thomasina was worthless. The way he spoke to her. The way he scowled at her. And now the way he was willing to bargain for a better price and sell her to a total stranger.

It had required every ounce of strength to not take this man down. Sean had actually broken into a sweat when her father had struck her. Sean's entire body locked up to keep from reacting. He had never had to work so hard to hold back his reaction. The man's behavior merited a beating and so much more. Yet he was her father.

Sean couldn't look at Thomasina. He didn't dare. She'd see the truth. No one deserved a father like this. No one. He felt pity for her. So here he was bartering with this horse's arse for his daughter. What would Sean do with her then? He had to protect her—one way or another. He could never let this strong spirited woman be at this man's mercy again. He'd break her for certain. How she'd survived this long was a miracle.

"All that I have is of great value to me." Sean received a frown for that answer. He wasn't certain where the idea had come from. "What do *ye* value?"

"What are ye asking?"

"Clearly ye dunna value yer own daughter."

"Of course I do. I value her greatly. It would only be a great debt that would have me parting with my lovely Tommy." He stopped to stab a finger toward Sean. "But that's only if she's a virgin still."

"Ye've been told she is."

Thomasina's father scowled at him and slapped his hand down in a dismissive gesture. "Enough!"

He turned away from Sean. His stomach dropped.

"Get on the horse, Tommy."

"Stop." Sean froze, afeared his desperation came through in his voice. He took a hard swallow. "I am not done with my offer."

The older man turned, his head shaking even before he started talking again. "Ye have nothing I can use. I need to have something of value."

"I have gold." Sean blurted it out without pausing to think first. His heart pounded faster. As fast as the desperation threatening to swamp him. "Ye'll not need to be taking the lass back."

Her father shook his head in a most pitying gesture. "Get another one, lad. She ain't worth it."

Sean's fist flew into the man's face and he landed hard on the ground, blood dripping from his nose.

"Dunna be talking that way about my betrothed." That felt good. A sense of peace settled in Sean's gut.

He walked past the man mumbling on the ground, mopping at the blood dripping down his chin. At least her father wasn't trying anything stupid. Sean touched Thomasina's arm ever so gently. She resisted when he tried to move her forward.

"Come with me, Thomasina." He paused, looking down into her face. Her eyes were wide but he couldn't tell if it was from the shock of him punching her father or at his calling her his betrothed. "Come with me."

A deep frown settled between her brows but she relented and went with him to Roana. He reached behind the saddlebag and withdrew the small sack.

"How much?" Sean felt like a heel asking how much he could buy Thomasina for but those were the rules of this travesty. He opened his bag then paused to turn and stare at the man who had suddenly managed to right himself.

"Well, I owe the man a goodly amount. Not sure as I ken the exact amount."

Sean tipped his head in irritation. "So ye've already given him her horse. That paid for some of the debt."

"Aye, but not a large part of it. I'm still quite bad off—"

"Tell me a number."

"It had been going on for quite a while so 'tis an extremely large—"

Sean raised his hand to silence him. He withdrew some coins, then threw the bag at Thomasina's father. The coins poured onto the ground but the older man caught the bag. He dropped to the floor, snatching up the coins like they were food and he hadn't eaten for a week.

"Now get on yer horse and be gone," Sean said.

"What about the other horse?"

"Nae! 'Tis nae longer yers."

The man shifted nervously as he counted the gold and silver, his mouth moving with each number.

"Do as I said." Sean was at the end of his rope. This man needed to leave or he was going to forget whose father he was and give him what he deserved. "I mean now."

Sean stepped closer and the man scrambled onto the top of his horse. The sack of coins tucked inside his tunic. "I'm going but..." Her father glanced at Thomasina. Was the man suddenly getting a conscience? "I would see her married."

"Nae!"

Her father stared at her long and hard before speaking. "Have ye no words of goodbye for yer old father?"

Thomasina trembled where she stood beside Sean. He wanted nothing more than to take her in his arms and comfort her.

"Goodbye."

"Ye dinna care what happened to her afore and now ye've lost the right. Go! And dunna come back to bother her again."

The older man snorted but headed the horse up the steep hill to the east. Thomasina returned to the cave without a word. Sean followed her.

"I'm sorry about all that." Sean needed to make amends but he didn't know how.

She turned on him. "Sorry? That ye own me now?"

He shook his head. "Nae! I am sorry that man is yer father."

Tears shimmered but she remained unmoving. "Now what are ye going to do with me?" She shook her head, her face crumbling. "I should have just gone with him and married the man."

A knife to the heart. He stepped closer, taking her chin in a tender grip, and urged her head up so he could look into her eyes. "Is that what ye wanted me to do? Let ye go off with him? Do as he ordered ye to?"

A tear slipped down her cheek. Her chin quivered. "I dunna ken."

She'd been through a lot. She needed comforting. Ever so gently, he wrapped his arms around her and pulled her against him. His chin rested on her head. She shook with her tears, her whole body moving against him. He stroked her back, careful not to think of her as a beautiful woman but as someone he could help. Like a sister. Yes. A sister.

After a while her tears subsided and he was quick to release his hold of her. "I think we should get something to eat in ye and then we can decide what we should do."

Sean moved to stoke up the fire. The dying embers quickly ignited the dried leaves he'd collected. He kept an eye on Thomasina who remained sitting on the floor facing the fire. She didn't appear to be looking at the fire but lost in her own memories.

"These fish are plentiful. I am quite adept at catching them."

He glanced her way, a fish in each hand, but she barely nodded in response. She was lost in her thoughts.

"I hope ye have a liking for fish. 'Tis less bloody than the little animals ye seemed to have an aversion to."

Something must have caught her attention because she turned to him. "How did ye ken that?"

He dropped his hands and smiled at her. "Ye could not bring yerself to watch me skin it. I tried to be quick."

She stood up, a frown on her lovely face, and came to stand beside him. "Ye cared how I felt?"

Sean's confusion was complete. What was it she was asking? "Yea! I cared and tried to not prolong yer discomfort."

She took the long stick poker he'd been using with the fire out of his hand. Wrapping his arm around her back, she pressed herself against his body. "Thank ye for yer kindness."

Thomasina tipped her head back, stood on tiptoe, and kissed him lightly on the cheek. "Ye are a special man. I want ye to ken that."

She withdrew and walked out of the cave. Sean kept her in his view as he cleaned the fish. She sat on a boulder a few feet from the mouth of the cave. The hill dropped off, creating a scenic view of dark hills and green forests. The birds chirped in the trees as if readying themselves to settle down for bed. Sean speared the fish and stuck the end into the ground so that they could stay over the fire to cook but not close enough to burn.

What had that been about? Of course he noticed how squeamish she behaved when he cleaned their supper. He feared she'd be sick but she wasn't. Instead she ate the meal with relish and thanked him for it. She appreciated everything he did for her. He, of course, gave her a hard time because he wanted her to remember she pretended to be a boy. He'd been terrible to her. Perhaps an apology was in order.

He wiped his hands on the cloth from his bag, smoothed his hair back, and headed toward the entrance. The sun was lowering in the west, an orange and pink display that gave the sky an unreal appearance. Thomasina stood by her horse now, stroking it with the hard brush.

Sean leaned against the opening, crossed his arms, and watched her a bit. He said, "Is that yer brush for the horse?"

"Yea. Niall made it for Daisy."

"Yer brother? Well done. Solid. And she enjoys the brushing." As if understanding their words, the horse pressed her snout into Thomasina's side.

"Yea." She didn't turn towards him but kept her attention focused on her animal.

"Thomasina, I want to explain why I'd been so hard on ye."

She turned toward him, a curious expression on her face.

"I knew ye were a girl—a woman—and I was trying to help ye to remember yer pretense of being a lad."

"Why dinna ye ask me why I was pretending?"

Sean felt again his knuckles grazing her breasts. Although he'd concentrated on not letting his face show what he knew, his desire had been to touch her again. He'd wanted to cup her breasts. To move in closer and feel their weight in his hands. To press against her nipple with his palm, encouraging its rigid response.

"I told ye. I dinna need to ken. It was yer decision."

She tightened her lips and stared at him.

He shifted under her perusal.

"Is that the only reason?"

He again saw her working so hard to get a large fire going despite the damp wood. His hands itching to stroke her round cheeks with every stretch. And when she bent over the fire, a burning desire to come up behind her, pull down those trews, and take her.

"Yea. Ye kept forgetting yer part."

"My part?" Her eyes were taking on the distinct look of displeasure. The eyebrows raising nearly to her hairline sounded like a death knell.

"Yea."

She stood abruptly and walked toward him, stopping close enough that he could take her in his arms and feast on her lovely, red lips. "I think ye knew I was a *woman* and ye were afraid of me."

Sean's jaw dropped. "What?"

"I think ye knew and ye were afraid to be with me as a woman and it was easier for *ye* to pretend I was a lad."

Air whooshed out of him like he'd been punched. She had it right. If he'd confronted her with the fact that she was a girl, he would have had to treat her differently. He would have needed to change his plans and accommodate her as the lady she was. He would have given in to his desire for her. He had chosen to pretend because it was safer.

The smell of burning fish startled them both and they hurried back into the cave. The charred fish hung by just a few pieces. Sean pulled the sticks out of the ground and dropped the food onto the rock. It sizzled, as did his fingers when he tried to get it off the stick the rest of the way.

Thomasina started to laugh when he cursed and stuck his finger in his mouth.

"Ye find humor in my pain? Please!" He indicated she try to get the burnt fish off the branch.

She cried out in pain when she suffered the same discomfort. Sean immediately took her hand and put her finger in his mouth. He licked his tongue against it as he'd done to his own. He hadn't expected her gasp. For the tiniest second he almost withdrew her finger but when he noticed her eyes closing slightly in a look that he'd swear was pleasurable, he stopped his reaction.

When she focused her eyes on him, he held her gaze. With the lightest grip, he held her hand and stroked her finger with his tongue. He parted his lips, removing the reddened appendage but continued his ministrations. Long, sweeping strokes. Her lips parted as she watched the movement. His cock was rock hard.

He turned her wrist up and kissed where her pulse beat. A light kiss. Then another. With each kiss, he drew her closer to him. He pulled her into his arms and against his length. He wrapped her arm around his back and lowered his lips to that little spot behind her ear, at the curve of her neck. She smelled of smoke and horses. Delicious. He kissed her there. She moaned as he knew she would.

"Ye like that?" He whispered the words then stroked her ear with his tongue. "Let me pleasure ye more."

She moved further into his arms but didn't answer him. He dropped his hand to her delectable bottom and caressed her with firm strokes that ended with him pulling her up against his hard length. His breath quickened.

"Does this give ye pleasure?"

"Yea."

Two hands firmly held her bottom. He was going to die if he didn't have her. He pushed his hardened tarse against her, undulating in the simulation of the act. "Mmm, I promise ye much pleasure." He kissed her by her ear. "Do ye want more?"

"Yea."

He reached up and held her chin, caressing the line of her jaw with his thumb. She opened her eyes, green and sparkling like precious gems. "Do ye ken what I am asking, mo mhíle stór?"

She nodded, her lips parting. Her eyes wide. Her breathing quick. All the signs of a woman ready to be taken.

"Let me make love to ye now."

On an exhale, she nodded again.

He took her mouth. Hot and sweet. He promised her pleasure. The lightness is his chest turned heavy. What did he know of pleasuring a virgin? It was the tried women who found his size appealing. They knew what they wanted and they took it from him. What if he went too fast or he frightened her with his size?

When she moaned against him, he was lost. All would be well. He would go slow, spending the entire night awakening her desires. Whatever it took, he would give her pleasure upon pleasure. His trip was suddenly taking on a much more enjoyable outcome.

Thomasina's desolation turned into a deep longing, a need that had to be met. Sean's rock hard body promised her so much. She wanted him. He was so large, she felt small in his arms. Like he tucked her into him. Protecting her. Lips firm and needy. He desired her. His hands caressing her, sending out waves of sensation. Pleasurable. Everywhere he touched her, he sparked a need in her. Low in her belly a flame grew. Lower still. When he rubbed his knuckles against the binding at her breast, she stilled.

"Yea, this needs to go."

He lifted one side of her tunic, exposing the material. With his teeth, he notched the material then ripped it up the side. He dropped the material to the ground then ran his hand over the material covering her now unbound breads. He cupped her breasts.

His lips were close to her ear. "Let me touch yer skin."

She nodded and he slipped his hand down her side to reach under her tunic. His hand on her bare skin made her jump where he caressed her ribs up to her breast. He held her closer as he grasped and released her.

"Coím. Never bind these again."

A flutter of anticipation rose in her belly. He found her desirable. Loosening his hold of her, he worked her tunic over her head, dropping it to the ground. As he had done earlier, he looked from one breast to the other, but now he ran his tongue over his lips. His eyes met hers.

"Ye have the most lovely breasts I've ever laid my eyes on."

He ducked his head and pressed his solid palm against her back, holding her close. He stroked her nipple with his tongue, then gently suckled. Desire like a jolt of lightning shot between her legs. She cradled his head against her and he drew her further into his mouth. His hand passed over the flat of her stomach to the juncture of her legs. Her breath caught. He stroked her with a firm hand. A hand that knew how to pleasure a woman. A hand that knew what she wanted. A hand that knew what she longed for. Wetness pooled.

He returned to her ear, his breath hot. "I want to be inside ye." He whispered the words as his hands worked their magic. "Ye want it, too."

Sean jerked away from her. She shivered at the cold air on her exposed body. Her eyes flew open.

"What are ye about?" Their kinsman and Niall's dearest friend, Lachlann, stood with a knife to Sean's throat. His green eyes wide as if he'd caught them in the actual act. A minute later and he would have.

Lachlann glanced at Thomasina. "Cover yerself lass!"

She jumped and grabbed up the tunic at her feet to obey. Her entire body heated with embarrassment. Her mouth dropped open but no words came out. After a minute she tried again. "What are ye—what are—where's Niall?"

"He's outside, lassie. And 'tis a damn good thing I caught ye rather than him." Lachlann yanked Sean back, the blade glistening. "Ye'll have some answering to do."

Sean held his hands open as if in surrender but said nothing. His eyes were on her. She shivered in response to his lust-filled look. He had a good six inches over Lachlann. She'd swear he allowed Lachlann to hold him. Then again the look on Lachlann's face was pure rage. He turned them both to face the entrance. She tugged at her tunic wishing it would cover her better.

Niall strode in and stopped abruptly. His friend, Aldred, had been following closely and plowed into his back. A bit shorter, his head received the brunt of it.

"What is amiss here?" Niall pointed to Sean. "Who is this?"

The blond man stopped rubbing his head where he'd smacked into Niall to peer around him. "I've never seen him before."

"Someone I found with yer sister!"

Niall's thick, red beard did little to hide his outrage as he stomped toward her. "Tommy! What is amiss?"

Her face crumbled and she fell into her brother's arms. "Oh, Niall. It was awful."

Sean made a strangled sound behind her.

"Tell me what the bastard has done to ye," Niall said in a tone as cold as stone.

She jerked away and glanced at Lachlann. Blood dripped from Sean's neck where the knife had broken his skin. He was going to kill him. "Stop!"

"Stop? Why? Tell us what he did to ye!" Niall's face suffused with color the same shade as his hair. "He will not be allowed to live if he has touched ye, Tommy."

Sean didn't move to defend himself but she felt certain he could. "Lachlann, yer slicing his neck open. Stop!"

The black-haired man smiled at her. "I'll cut off more than his head if he's forced himself on ye."

"Nae! He dinna force himself on me." She pulled at his arm. Sean's hand wrapped around her middle as if he stood there on his own without a care. "Release him!"

Niall had his broadsword pointed toward Sean. "Go on, Lachlann, let him go."

Sean righted himself and dabbed at his neck. His fingers came back covered with his own blood. Although his lips thinned into an angry line, he didn't speak.

"So what is amiss here?" Lachlann's irritation apparent in his tone. "I come in here and he has his hand between yer legs, suckling yer breasts—"

Sean jerked out of his clutches and turned about to punch him squarely in the face. Lachlann's head jerked back at the impact but he remained standing. He covered his face as blood dripped from his lips, oozing between his fingers. "Shite. His fist is like iron."

"Dunna open yer mouth again," Sean said.

Lachlann's eyes widened but he nodded.

Sean turned toward Thomasina. "Are ye well? Should I speak or would ye rather?"

Thomasina's confusion must have shown on her face because Sean gave a nod and turned to her brother. Closing the distance between them despite the sword Niall held pointed at him, Sean said, "I was about to make love to my betrothed."

iall's expression went from shocked, as if unable to comprehend Sean's words, to horrified that what he'd heard him say was actually true, to disbelief that it might actually be true. He doubled over as he laughed uncontrollably. For quite a while. The sound wore on Thomasina's nerves. Sean looked absolutely livid but didn't speak at first.

Glancing at Thomasina with narrowed eyes, he seemed to be assessing how she took her brother's behavior. She expected no less from him at such a statement since he was so protective.

"Is this yer brother? Are ye certain, Thomasina? The one ye came to for help?"

That received an immediate reaction. Niall stood up, a scowl on his face now. "What are ye asking?"

"Ye're acting like an arse." Lachlann spoke up from where he stood with his hip perched against the boulder, still wiping at his lip. "Ye're acting like her being betrothed is an absurd idea. We all knew it was just a matter of time with her beauty."

Lachlann smiled toward her then grimaced at the pain from his split lip. He was a sweetheart and the only friend of Niall's that she would not feel ashamed of having been seen naked in front of.

"Thank ye, Lachlann."

Sean glanced between the two of them. "*Is* he laughing because he thinks no one would want ye? Is he daft?"

Thomasina's face heated. Her brother was her biggest supporter. Their sire was just as cruel to Niall but knew where to draw the line with him. He needed Niall.

Niall pushed out his chest and moved in closer to Sean. "Let me just say I dunna think the only daughter of the MacDonnell Clan would marry someone from across the sea."

Thomasina shoved her hair over her shoulder and began pacing. "'Tis not like that, Niall." She turned toward Sean and continued, "And I dunna think 'tis exactly as he said it."

Sean frowned and crossed his arms, even puckering his lips for effect, and made as if he tried to remember something. His expression dropped with his arms and he nodded. "Nae. 'Tis exactly as I said it. Ye're my betrothed."

"Why? Because ye gave my father money for me?"

"Tommy! Nae!" Niall said.

His sympathetic tone started the tears. "It was awful, Niall. He came here and started saying terrible things about me."

Her brother took her in his strong embrace. She turned her face into his shoulder and let the tears take over.

"Shhh"

"It was the O'Reilly he betrothed me to."

Niall pulled away at that. "Not that whoreson. That man's been after ye since ye were just a girl. I saw the attention he gave ye and even at two and ten, I ken it was wrong. When I told father about it, he could not clear his mind enough to understand me." He shook his head and turned toward his kinsmen. "I was afeared for her."

"Aye, ye did. We made a vow to never leave her alone with the man," Aldred said. His stern expression spoke of the seriousness of the offense.

Thomasina shivered, relieved to have no memory of the events.

"That's why I decided to go back to Uncle Garnait." He glanced at Sean. "He took over as clan leader when our father fell into a drunken stupor. We were nearly all murdered in our sleep when an enemy snuck in under his nose."

Thomasina saw no acknowledgement from Sean, just silence.

"I canna believe the old man would do this to ye," Niall said.

Niall's pained expression pulled at Thomasina. Her brother had been through a lot trying to look out for them when they were shunned.

"He lost everything," she said. "He had nothing else to offer him."

Niall gave her his full attention. "And he doesna have ye. He canna just give ye away like ye're something to barter. Just because he's lost all that is rightfully his doesna mean yer nothing but some goods he can trade out."

Thomasina sniffled and wiped at her nose. "But he did. First he gave the man Daisy. And when that was not enough, he gave him me."

Niall looked heavenward, closed his eyes, and shook his head as if asking for strength. He faced her again. "Apologies for not being there for ye. I'm here now. What would ye have me do?"

Sean chose that moment to move in closer. "I dunna ken exactly what ye're speaking of but I meant what I said. I'm taking the lass to wife."

Niall's jaw dropped at the same time as her own. Sean's stoic expression revealed nothing. No feelings of tenderness. No feelings of deep longing. No feelings of anything. Thomasina recovered first.

"Nae, Sean. Ye dunna have to do that. Niall will see to things."

Sean seemed to still, even his chest stopped rising. He looked at her as if he were seeing her anew. Searching her face, he lifted his hand toward her but dropped it before he touched her. He glanced down, then walked out of the cave.

"I dunna think that was the best way to handle this, Tom." Lachlann pushed away from the boulder and followed the man. He indicated for Aldred to come as well.

"What should I have said?" Thomasina asked Niall.

The horse snorting outside the cave had Niall and Thomasina following as well. Sean now sat fully clothed on the horse, his sword strapped to the saddle. Her heart leapt into her throat.

Without so much as a glance her way, he said. "I've seen ye to yer brother. I'll be on my way now."

"Wait!" Thomasina couldn't breathe. "What are ye doing on Daisy?"

Sean took a deep breath and sighed, bent his knee in his saddle to rest his elbow there. He faced Niall.

"I've been trying to explain to yer sister that I paid for the use of this horse during my time here. My time has come to an end. I will be returning the horse and getting back what I put up for collateral. Nothing about that has changed."

He still didn't look at her but returned to straddling the horse. Kneeing the animal, Sean urged it to the path that wound down the side of the mountain.

"Ye're just leaving?" Thomasina started after him but Niall pulled her back.

"Let him go, Tommy."

It was hard for her to catch her breath. "Nae! He canna just leave me."

"Why not?" Lachlann's eyes pierced hers.

"Well, he—he has my horse."

Lachlann stroked her hair. "We'll get the horse back."

She watched until he was out of sight then strained for any sound. She listened to hear him leaving her. Sean was gone. Going back to Eire and .. she never learned what it was he went back for. He'd given away his wealth to save her and now he was gone.

"Oh, Niall. I've done something terrible."

Niall and Lachlann exchanged glances but neither spoke.

"I canna just stand here and have him… leave."

Lachlann urged her back into the cave with an arm around her shoulder. "Why not, Tommy? He said he'd done as ye'd asked."

She halted inside. "Nae. Ye dunna understand. There was more. He…"

Thomasina closed her eyes and took a calming breath. How much did they need to know? Lachlann had witnessed their intimacy so at least he knew that much. Sean had given up much for her. That was what they needed to know. She opened her eyes to find both men watching her. Her lips twitched into a smile but her stomach felt like a rock had been deposited there.

"Let's sit," she said.

Niall shook his head. No one budged. "Ye need to tell me what ye're trying to not tell me."

"I'm not trying to not tell ye anything."

"Oh yea ye are and I ken it, Tommy. That's the look ye get when ye're preparing for prevarication."

Her heart lurched. Sean had said she prevaricated, too. She turned back to the woods he'd disappeared in. She felt empty.

"I told ye I found her in a compromising situation."

She spun around at that. Lachlann watched her even as he spoke to Niall.

"Ye started to say—"

"Nae! Dunna discuss me as if I'm not right here. Nothing happened that I dinna want to have happen."

Niall's eyes widened, his expression seemed frozen with fear. "Tell me what ye've done, Tommy."

Fear fluttered in her stomach at the look. "'Tis not what ye think."

"What is it I think?"

"That he made love to me." Thomasina's eyes closed as her mind remembered how close they'd come. Yes, she had wanted him to make love to her, to hold her in his strong arms, and show her all that... pleasure.

She opened her eyes to find Niall almost nose to nose with her.

"Stop trying to lie to me!"

Lachlann drew Niall back. When he finally stopped glaring at her and turned to him, Lachlann gave a little shake of his head. Giving his full attention to Thomasina now, Lachlann gave her his best attentive expression. Stepping a bit closer, the small line between his eyes deepened. "So tell us what we dunna ken."

"Thank ye. When father came here—" *He caught me in Sean's arms.* No, better not to say that. "He demanded to ken if I was still a virgin."

Niall scowled. "Why would he think ye were not?"

Oh did she need to tell him? No!

"Ye ken how father is. He always thinks the worst of me."

"That's true enough. I'm sorry, Tom." Niall stroked her cheek.

The memory of Sean's hand on her cheek made her heart clench.

"So tell me what ye said to him."

"Well... Sean punched him in the face."

Niall, Lachlann and Aldred stood stock still, as if shocked speechless, then started laughing. Loud, uncontainable laughter.

Thomasina gave a little laugh as well. "It was sort of funny, to see him knocked on his arse."

"He's done it to me enough," Niall said as he struggled to catch his breath. "Ah, that Sean has balls of steel."

"He does! And a fist to match," Lachlann added, grabbing his jaw where the man had punched him.

They started laughing again. It took them a long moment to realize she wasn't joining this time.

"Sean is a good man."

They sobered and exchanged concerned looks again.

"We dinna say he was not. He may indeed be a *good* man," Niall said. "He's just not the *right* man."

"How do ye ken?" Thomasina whirled around and left them in the cave.

She gazed off the way Sean had gone. He wouldn't be back. They had dismissed him and he'd done nothing to defend himself. He'd done nothing to change their mind. He'd done nothing like profess his deepest desire was to marry her.

"I thought he cared for me." Thomasina whispered this time.

Someone came up behind her and she brushed a tear from her cheek. Lachlann put a comforting arm around her, pulling her close to his side. "I'm thinking ye may be sweet on the man."

She shook her head but the tears kept sliding down her face.

"Tom, dunna try to lie to me. *I* saw ye with him. Ye were lost in his arms." He spoke in a quiet voice and stressed the words that tugged at her heart. "Ye were impassioned." He turned her to face him. "Ye were ready to have him love ye. The deed would be done now if I had not interrupted."

"Oh, I did. I wanted him to love me." She whispered the words like a shared secret. "I've never felt anything so strong as that before."

He brushed her hair away from her face. "Are ye certain it was the man and not that… maybe ye're just ready to be a wife?"

"I never cared about being a wife. I never even thought about it. But being wrapped in arms so strong I felt... like a boat safe in a harbor. Like I'd found my home. Never before. Not until Sean touched me."

"Do ye think that was what he might have been after all along?" His words were so quiet, as if afraid to hurt her with any accusations.

"Oh Lachlann. Nae. He's not like that." She shook her head, pleading with her voice for him to understand. "He's a good man. He is strong, a warrior, but he was kind with me."

She looked down at herself then continued. "I was dressed like this, like a boy." She smiled at him. "I'm not very well endowed so it was simple enough but he saw through my disguise and protected me."

Lachlann frowned. "Then why are ye still disguised?"

"Well, he didn't admit he knew I was a girl. He let me keep acting... like... a boy. What?"

Lachlann's full brow dipped into an angry frown. "Oh he did? And did ye end up in any unexpected situation with him? Like a bed? Or a swim in a loch?"

"Nae!"

"He dinna see you soaked to the bone and yer bonny body all revealed?"

"Why would ye even think that?"

Lachlann's brows raised and his eyes opened wide as if caught saying too much. He turned a bright shade of red.

"Did ye have a... situation like that?"

"Well, not intentional—Never mind me!" His embarrassment was making him sharp with her.

She smiled. "Nae. He made suggestions about how I could be more like a lad."

"Such as?" That hint of accusation was still there.

"I should not be squeamish... and defensive. And I should definitely want to learn swear words—"

"Enough!" Lachlann lifted his hand. "Did he take advantage of ye as a lad since he knew ye were a lass?"

She shook her head. "Never. He protected me. He protected me at the inn when the serving wench figured out I was a girl. He protected me when I walked in on the Norman soldiers raping her. He protected me when—" Sobs tightened her throat. "—when they were slaughtering the soldiers."

Thomasina had no idea why she sobbed uncontrollably but was relieved Lachlann took her in his arms, his hand caressing her back in a soothing motion. He seemed to understand.

"I'd say ye have it bad."

She pressed her face into his chest and decided she didn't know, and didn't want to know, what he was talking about. She just wanted it to be gone.

"And when father was here and tried to take me away, Sean gave him his coins. All of them."

Lachlann stilled his movements.

"He told our father *he* was my betrothed now… that I was a bonny lass he'd not be leaving."

"So?" Niall came up behind them without a sound.

Lachlann kept his arms around her but she struggled to get herself under control.

"I think we have to get the man back," Lachlann said.

"Nae! 'Tis not to be done this way."

She started to pull away and face her brother but Lachlann held her fast.

"Dunna be an arse. Look at her! She's heartbroken."

"Dunna ye understand? There's to be an arrangement with the clan further north. She's to marry one of their sons."

"That's not what her heart is telling her."

Thomasina stilled at his words. Had she really said that? Lachlann relaxed his arms when she tried to pull away this time.

"What are ye saying, Lachlann? I only told ye Sean was a good man." She wiped her nose and turned to face her brother. "I'll not be losing ye only chance to get back into the clan, Niall. I promise ye."

Niall glanced over her head to look at Lachlann before looking at the ground. He kicked at the dirt but neither of them spoke.

"When father came, he was dragging me away and telling me I'd better still be a virgin or O'Reilly would not be accepting me anymore." Her voice grew quiet. "Sean threw his bag of coins at him. He ordered him to leave and not come back."

Niall kept his eyes on her as she spoke, a dark expression on his face. He heaved a big sigh then looked at Lachlann.

"I'd say we ken what we're to do then." Lachlann was the first to break the silence. "Dunna ye agree, Niall?"

"Yea, yer judgment is sound. Let's see if we can track the man down."

"Sean?" Thomasina's fluttering started again, like a butterfly set free to visit the flowers. "He's going to the village. That's where he's gone."

Niall cupped her face with a gentle hand then smiled. "Ye're a wonderful lass, Thomasina, we willna be giving ye up to anyone who doesna realize that. Ye ken?"

She closed her eyes but didn't speak. He was giving his blessing and she felt she'd been given another chance at life. Finally, she looked at him. "Ye can judge for yerself. I'll not gainsay ye."

Lachlann put a hand on each of their shoulders. "Then I'd say we've some riding to do."

CHAPTER 10

Sean traveled through the night at a fast pace, as fast as he could accomplish without breaking his neck from a fall. The moon cast the road in enough light to pass without problem. Roana was a sturdy, wise animal who moved carefully among the outcroppings along the trail. He hadn't even noticed the difficulty of the path when he'd held Thomasina asleep in his arms. The rise and fall of her chest as she slept, oblivious to all around. Overwhelmed by the bloodshed, she'd found an escape in sleep. He'd held her fast to him, protecting her with his body as he'd done at the inn. As he would gladly have continued to do for the rest of his days.

Pain shot through his chest as if it had been slammed into by an axe. Surely his heart was breaking in two. He'd been so close to having her. When did the feelings he had for Thomasina become ingrained in his gut? He'd ridiculed and tormented her the whole time while inside he'd marveled at her strength, at her fortitude, at her courage. She was an amazing woman.

That moment at the inn when she went into a panic thinking that everyone knew she was a woman. The reality that he needed her to be strong for *him* had swamped him. He'd not acknowledged it. He even convinced himself he just needed a good fuck but she was in him even then. That he had been able to calm her, to instill her with faith in herself, to trust herself even—that had been exhilarating. Without him even knowing it, he'd made the decision to be there for her, however she wanted him. That was his fatal mistake.

The only daughter of some northern clan couldn't marry a warrior from Eire. She'd seemed like a lost soul whose father had laid aside any desire to guard her and see her well married. A man lost in drink and wasting away. Sean knew that well enough. She seemed to feel something for Sean even though she'd never said it. Was it out of fear that she clung to him? That she accepted his touch? That she had wanted him to make love to her?

A groan escaped from the depths of his soul. A single wolf in the distance answered him. Clouds passed in front of the moon, casting him in darkness. He urged the horse to stop then jumped down to lead the way between the trees.

"I'll see ye safe, Roana. All is well. Sun up will be here anon."

On foot, the road seemed endless. By daybreak, he'd found shelter at a fallen tree and slept. Haunted by strange dreams of being chased by some unknown foe. An animal. The animal became the soldier with the scarred face. He held a knife to Sean's throat. The sensation of having his throat sliced open woke him with a gasp covered in sweat. He grabbed at his throat. Still intact. The cold air worked into his clothing and he shivered uncontrollably. A light dusting of snow had fallen while he slept. The sun was high in the sky. He felt exhausted.

Standing to stretch, he called to Roana with the whistle Thomasina had used. She came immediately, rubbing her nose against his outstretched hand.

"Glad I've not been abandoned by ye as well."

Roana snorted in answer. Her ears twitching, she tipped her head up, bumping him twice as if to direct him to the area further up the hill. The path they'd been following no longer visible but he saw nothing untoward.

"Methinks ye must have had a nasty dream as well, my friend."

He mounted the animal and urged her forward with a general pull to the right. Hopefully the animal knew which way the town lay. By gloaming, they'd arrived. It was quite a busy place, overrun with Normans. Their mail and shields indicated these were more than common soldiers making patrols. Calls and shouts carried across the inlet as they moved about at their important duty. Investigating the slaughter at the inn, no doubt. Sean planned to stay clear of all the goings-on. He walked Roana to the blacksmith.

"Hail!"

No response from within.

The place was cold and empty. Sean could clearly see the coffer where the man had put Tadhg's knife for safe keeping. It was unlocked. He brought Roana around back to see to feeding and watering her. She was a good animal and would hopefully be back with her owner afore long. Thomasina's smiling, green eyes flashed through his mind. He jerked the saddle off her back and headed inside the lean-to. Several misshapen iron horseshoes and a hooded suit of mail lay on the bench beside the bellows that hung beside the cold hearth.

He stopped within the darkened space and looked around. The blacksmith was nowhere to be seen.

"Anyone here?" Sean spoke a little louder but didn't wish to call undue attention to himself.

The soldiers moved along the buildings outside in twos and threes, swords in hand as if hunting down prey. Sean swallowed. They seemed intent on catching whoever they were searching for. He wondered how it would all turn out but doubted the men who came in with Ivan would ever be caught. That wasn't the usual way these things went. The Saxons would all protect the killers because they didn't want the Normans here either.

Once Roana was brushed down and settled in, Sean gave one last look around for the blacksmith. He went to the coffer, dropped his items beside it, and lifted the lid. Swords, helmets, and trinkets filled the space. Tadhg's prized knife with the blade that swiveled from either side lay tucked between two helms. Sean picked it up.

"Hey! What are you about?" A man's voice boomed.

Sean jerked around, knife in hand, to face the man who had rented him the horse.

"Hail! I've returned the horse I borrowed. I was retrieving my knife. Ye were nowhere to be found."

The man nodded, recognition crossing his face. "Aye. My thanks. Any problems with her?"

"No, she's a sound animal."

"Sorry about your lying little friend—"

"Stay!" A soldier stood in the opening behind the blacksmith. "Drop your weapon."

Sean was confused who he gave the order to since neither he nor the blacksmith were holding a weapon. He glanced at the treasured knife. Suddenly understanding, he hunkered down to place the knife carefully on the ground. The soldier closed the distance, another one followed close behind, and hit the hilt against the side of Sean's head. He saw stars, grabbed at his head, and tumbled over onto the ground. The man kicked him with his tackety boot. Sharp pain shot through Sean's hip. The two soldiers jerked him to standing.

"So we've found you, you devil spawn."

Sean opened his eyes but had trouble focusing on the soldier, his recognizable helmet and nose guard told him all he needed to know.

"I dunna ken what ye're talking about."

The soldiers glanced at each other and laughed as they yanked him up tighter between them. "A huge man with long, blond hair. I'd say this is the man."

"What man?" Sean asked. His arms felt about to come out of their sockets.

The Normans dragged him into the street where more soldiers gathered to watch, their swords at the ready. Sean dare not fight but he caught sight of Tadhg's knife being stepped on by the soldiers who came up behind his two assailants.

"Please." Sean dug his heals in to try and stop the men from dragging him.

One of the nearby Normans stepped forward to plant his sword hilt into his stomach. Sean doubled over in pain. The soldiers on either side jerked him back up.

"Of what am I being accused?"

One man dressed in leather and mounted on a black destrier watched from the shadow of a tree to the right, his dark eyes locked onto Sean. He leaned toward someone who stood beside the horse. "Is this the man you saw?"

Sean struggled to see the other man. Sweat dripped down his face, blurring his vision but it was a small man. No higher than the horse, wearing dark clothing. A cloak—the air *whooshed* out of Sean.

Ivan!

"Aye, that's the one I saw. Like a mad man swinging his swords around the good Norman soldiers, hacking them to their death."

"What?" Sean strained against the grip of the men leading him forward. "I've done no such thing."

Another soldier paused in front of him. With a deep scowl he looked Sean up and down then punched him in the face. The men on either side held him fast. They laughed and then the soldier punched him again. Sean yanked against the viselike grip the two men had of him. The man punched him again. And again.

Sean awoke on the ground, his bloodied face in the sand. The feet of several soldiers surrounding him. For a moment he feigned he was still asleep. A kick to his side was followed by a bucket of sea water poured over his head.

"Get up!" It was the man in leather now standing in front of him. His hands fisted at his hips, his feet in a wide stance. The Norman lord.

Sean's face stung where the salt water mixed in with his blood. His arms tied behind him now, the two soldiers yanked him to standing. He searched for Ivan among the crowd that had formed around them but could not find him.

The scowl on the lord's face spoke of the rage within. He was lord here. There was no reason to hold back. His word was law. A Norman lord who could condemn Sean to death right here on the word of that scoundrel, Ivan. Sean had no defense. No way of disproving whatever lie Ivan had made up about him.

"My lord—"

"Silence!" The powerful lord shook with his fury. "You dare not speak in your defense. We have an eye witness against you. He *saw* you slaughter my soldiers—my son." The man's voice broke.

Sean's heart pounded as if trying to break free of his chest. His breathing heaved as if he'd run miles. A hooded man with a massive chest came to stand beside Sean. Two gloved hands gripped a massive two-handed sword. The beheading sword.

Sweat poured from Sean, mixing with the sand and dirt as it dripped down his face. Memories swam through his mind. The dark green of his homeland. The smell of honeysuckle in the spring. The taste of roasted duck. He'd wasted his time.

The soldiers behind shoved him down, forcing him to his knees.

He wished he'd not spent so much of his life pining over Brighit.

"My son was killed by your butchery—then branded like an animal." The lord's mouth twisted with the angry words.

He should have listened to Brighit. They were not meant to be together. He could have been married to another, perhaps with children by now.

"I found him bleeding to death—" The lord struck Sean across the side of the face with a leather strap.

Blood pooled in his mouth and Sean spit it out. What he felt for Thomasina was so different than what he'd felt for Brighit.

"—My son was a valiant soldier. He'd fought with honor—"

Sean again saw the Norman soldier with the scarred face. He'd had the scars of battle. The hooded man readied his feet, twitching his fingers as he gripped and re-gripped the hilt of his sword.

"—He didn't deserve to be hacked down by the likes of you."

Sean closed his eyes in silent prayer to a God he wasn't certain would listen. He swallowed, stiffened his shoulders, and then said, "Nae. Yer son, William, did not deserve to die like that."

His breath lay trapped in his chest as he waited for the lord to respond. Thomasina's face came to him, filling the void in the silence. The way she'd looked right before he kissed her, when he'd taken her into his arms, when he was about to make love to her.

"What do you know of my William?" the man's voice boomed.

Sean opened one eye, the other stuck shut, struggling to see the man through the blood and sweat dripping down his face. "I ken he was a soldier. I ken he'd always fought hard. I ken he was a man I'd raise no hand against if not in battle."

The lord's face suffused with color. His eyes nearly bugged out of his head as he struggled. Struggled with the pain, the loss, and the revelation that Sean may not be his killer.

"My lord, I didna kill yer son. I swear it." Sean's voice quiet, his heart throbbed in his throat.

The lord ducked down close, his face mere inches from Sean's. "Why. Should. I. Believe. You?"

"I am a warrior. I would *never* hack down a soldier."

"The little man said he saw you."

"The little man is a liar. I'd venture a guess that he is the one who provoked the massacre."

"How do you know that?"

Sean hesitated. He didn't want to admit he did nothing to help the soldiers. That would be reason enough to justify his beheading.

The lord stood up. He had already made his decision.

"Commence the beheading!" The lord returned to his warhorse.

Sean couldn't breathe.

The beheading sword raised.

Sean's life meant nothing.

The hooded man grunted.

This was the end.

"Sir Peter of Normandy will vouch for me." Sean's words tripped up together as they spilled out on his pent up breath.

The hooded man bent back, his arms high over his head.

The lord lifted his hand and Sean closed his eyes. Too late.

The hooded man took a breath.

"Cease!"

Sean tightened in preparation for his head being sliced from his body. A whoosh passed his ear. He waited for the pain. There should be pain.

The hooded man panted beside him.

Sean heard him. He opened his eyes. His head still in place. The beheading sword impaled the ground just in front of him.

"You know Sir Peter?" the lord spoke again.

"Yea! Peter is… a kinsmen of my clan. He's married the leader's daughter."

"Where did you see him last?"

"It was at the Priory south of York. They were about to lay siege to the castle there." Sean searched his brain for any detail that would stay his execution. "He was with Sir John."

"Was the king with them?"

"Nae. King William had been delayed and they were to lay siege in anticipation of his arrival. They gave me leave to return home."

One chance to save his neck.

"To Eire?"

"Yea, my lord." Mayhap an opportunity to make amends for all his errors. He didn't want to beg. "My lord, if ye would but send word, Sir Peter would be my witness."

The lord perused the crowd surrounding him. They were all his to command and all eyes were on him. The entertainment of a good beheading was not lost on the lord. No doubt he weighed their anticipated disappointment. Sean swallowed.

The lord straightened himself, squaring his shoulders, then with one slight tip of his head he said, "To the pillory then."

Sean exhaled then drew in a sweet breath. And another. He would live to see another day.

The hooded man stepped toward the lord. Sean's heart dropped to his stomach.

"My lord! If he is brethren to Sir Peter and their clan is held in high esteem by King William, perhaps we need only to shackle him rather than subject him to a public punishment?"

Sean's entire body began to shake with relief.

"See it done." The lord mounted his horse. His shoulders rounding again. "And send a messenger on to York."

The soldiers who had nearly yanked Sean's arms from his body, helped him to his feet with gentler motions now.

"Get some water." The beheading man gave the orders. He wrapped an arm around Sean's torso. "And some food."

Sean stiffened at the gesture. "My thanks."

"I'm just glad I was able to save your neck."

Sean studied the leather-covered head with deep, brown eyes barely visible through the two eye holes and started laughing. Pain ripped through his torso and he immediately regretted it.

He said, "As am I."

CHAPTER 11

Niall, Lachlann, Aldred and Thomasina had arrived just as the beheading was about to commence. They had walked toward the gathering of townsmen. Thomasina could make out a well-dressed man on a horse in the center. The local lord. She'd pressed in between a tiny, gray-haired woman and a man with a large, ugly lump on the side of his neck. A huge man was shoved to his knees, barely able to keep from falling. The broad shoulders. The long hair down his back. Her heart began to race.

Her jaw dropped. Her gasp cut off by Lachlann's hand covering her mouth. He'd lifted her clear off the ground to carry her in the opposite direction. She'd twisted against his hold and did her best to kick him anywhere she could make contact. Her fighting instinct surprised her but not him. He'd been ready. Niall and Aldred had stayed behind. All she knew was she had to save Sean. Lachlann carried her deep into the woods where they'd left their horses and refused to release her.

The sobbing started immediately, from deep inside. Some well of emotion began to spew and she couldn't control it. Lachlann turned to cradle her in his arms.

"Shhh."

"Nae. Nae, they canna kill him."

"Wait. Wait and see what Niall finds out."

"He'll be dead. We're too late."

"Shh, now. I dunna believe ye found the man just to have him ripped away from ye."

"Ye're wrong. He's dead."

Niall and Aldred burst through the trees and dropped in an exhausted heap at her feet. Niall shook his head.

"Nae—" He gasped for air. "He's not dead."

Lachlann released his hold and she threw herself at Niall, grabbing at his tunic. "Tell me! Is he safe?"

"I dunna… something about Peter."

Lachlann's face screwed up in confusion. "Brighit's Peter?"

Niall took a few deep gulps of air. "Nae. Yea! They were going to kill him but he mentioned Peter of Normandy… he said they were south of York."

Lachlann's eyes widened. "Then they are the same. How does he ken them?"

All eyes turned to Thomasina. She shrugged. "He didna tell me much of himself."

Niall blew a steady breath. "Let me think. He said Peter was kinsman to their clan." He turned to Thomasina. "He is from Eire?"

"Yea. That's where he was going when I took my horse back."

They stared at her. They didn't ask the obvious, she decided not to elaborate, and they turned to each other.

"Brighit was from Eire." Lachlann's eyebrows rose with his speculation. "And we did think the men with her might have abducted her."

Aldred scratched the whiskers on his chin. "Something wasna right there, that's true enough."

"Yea, then we found her with Peter and they were under attack." Niall laughed. "I dunna ken what that was about."

"But ye and Aldred brought the little man and his friends to the coast for Peter, did ye not?" Lachlann's tone held his disbelief. "Did they say *nothing*?"

"We were not listening to their blathering. We were glad to be rid of him," Niall said.

"Ye had the better end of the trade with that little fox hugging ye the whole way to Tanshelf." Aldred's wide eyes and raised brows accused Lachlann right back.

Lachlann grinned. "Aye, she was a fair lass with her auburn hair and huge, brown eyes. And her bre—"

Thomasina glared at him. "So what of the man named Peter? Sean said he knew him?"

"So he must be from Brighit's clan in Eire. Mayhap he was here for her?"

Thomasina's heart lurched at the idea of Sean coming all this way for some woman named Brighit.

"He said Peter would vouch for him. They sent messengers to York so he is safe for the time being."

~

Sean sat with his legs secured by a heavy chain threaded through a solid iron hook driven into the ground. He'd spent the first hour trying to pull the thing out the ground. Then half the night using the chain itself as a lever. He'd yanked up with a steady force until his arms could no longer handle the heavy weight. The thing hadn't moved.

He lifted one leg as far as he could without causing the other to move. It was quite an ingenuous device. He had several yards of chain if he kept one foot close to the post but if he pulled it through, he could shuffle around it.

The ground was hard and cold. His limbs were cramping up. He had been smelling meat roasting for an hour now. His stomach continued to growl. He scooted back and leaned his shoulder against the tree stump behind him. It was going to be a long day.

A bat flew out from the trees to his left. He leaned forward and waited. A small dark figure emerged from the forest. It seemed to drift toward him, shifting in the darkness. He rubbed his tired eyes.

"Leave me. I've nothing more to tell ye." Sean leaned back again.

"Nothing to say to me?"

Ivan.

Outrage washed over him. Sean jumped to his feet, wincing as pain shot through every part of his battered body. He turned to the man who was just now visible. "Ye dare show yer face?"

Ivan stopped just shy of Sean being able to reach him.

"Why not?" Ivan opened his upturned hands. "You are a man. I am a man. We have much in common."

"We have nothing in common. Ye're the worst kind of man. Ye're a scoundrel, not even a man."

"Why? Because I turned you in?"

"Yea, we call that bearing false witness where I come from." Sean was surprised at his own unexpected outburst. He wasn't the best Christian but apparently he listened to something the village priest said.

"'Tis where I come from as well." Ivan tipped his head. "I just believe the ends may justify the means."

"Ye'll burn in hell." Sean faced straight ahead.

Ivan shook his head with deliberation before he spoke. "I'm not certain you understand the tight spot you're in here."

He paused as if waiting to see if Sean would respond. He did not.

"No messengers have been sent to York. There will be no word from Peter of Normandy."

Sean turned toward him at that. The enormity of the situation sunk into his tired brain. The Normans wanted him dead.

"The soldiers believe they have their man. And I, naturally, reassured them when they came to question me yet again."

Sean's sense of his surroundings intensified. The smell of the dung heap. The moss growing along the well. The ocean waves in the distance. He ground his teeth together to keep from responding. The fear coiling in his belly would surely be heard in his voice.

"Nothing to say? Well," Ivan reached beneath his cloak and withdrew a heavy metal object, "I have something to say."

The key to Sean's leg iron. Ivan held it up in front of him like a carrot before a stubborn mule. Sean still refused to speak. If he didn't speak, Ivan could only guess how he'd be feeling. Sean felt angry enough to rip the man's head from his body with his two bare hands.

"I understand you may have... acted hastily when confronted by all that bloodshed."

Sean shifted. Ivan smiled.

"Come now, even a warrior can have too much. Yes? And that sweet little morsel you held in your arms? Mmm, a piece of that would be worth getting away for."

Rage swept like a fire through his chest and Sean lunged at the man. Ivan stepped back, his eyes widening in fear. He snorted then laughed when he realized he was beyond Sean's grasp.

"Now. Now. That's no way to behave. And me with the key to your freedom? Should I just leave you here?"

Sean's lungs were ready to bust. If no one was going to come to save him, he would need to save himself. It hadn't set well with him to be chained like this. Waiting.

"What do ye want?" Sean asked.

"Ah, now, you see? We can speak as men."

Sean's jaw ached from keeping his mouth shut. He gave the slightest nod.

"I knew you would see reason." Ivan sat on the ground, just beyond Sean's reach. He glanced up at him. A questioning expression.

Sean acquiesced and sat back down.

Ivan smiled again. The greasy smile of someone who was going to sell you something you didn't want, at a price you couldn't pay. "Good. Now, as I see it, you have every reason to want to agree to any bargain that can save your neck. Would I be correct?"

Sean nodded again.

"Well, let me explain my bargain." The smile dropped from the little man's face. "You will side with my Lord Godwin against these Normans and kill as many as need be."

"Godwin?"

"Yes." Ivan rolled his eyes as if Sean were the biggest idiot he'd ever come upon. "*He* is the rightful king. He is the only living male heir to the

House of Godwin and nephew to King Harold who was overthrown by William."

"I thought all Godwins were killed in battle. How did he survive the fighting?"

Ivan shifted, averting his eyes. Ah, a touchy subject.

This time Sean was the one who smiled. "Or should I be asking how did he avoid fighting?"

"Lord Leofrid does not need your condescension." Ivan's tone was thick with contempt. "He was not in the country when the attack happened."

Many of the Godwins had been exiled to Eire over the years. Other clans welcomed them in. Perhaps family. For generations, the MacNaughton had always stayed clear of the power struggles going on across the water. Whether Danes, Gaels, or Saxons, they weren't worth the trouble.

"It was more than an attack, Ivan. It was an ongoing battle. For months."

"Yes but his father, Tostig, was quickly overrun both by his own brother and then the relentless Normans. They had no chance."

"So how is it different now? The Normans are the ones who have all the power."

Ivan smiled, his fat tongue gliding over his lips before he spoke. "Because now Leofrid has the backing of the MacLochlainn."

"Of Inishowen? That's quite a ways to go to get support for a cause over here."

"There are others. Across Eire. But MacLochlainn has the thirst for power. The guts for the venture. They enjoy the fighting. Norman blood will spill until it runs like a river through the streets. Leofrid will be crowned king and their alliance—the Saxons and the Eire—will be too powerful for anyone to stop us."

Ivan paused to catch his breath, his shoulders rising and falling with each gulp of air. He wiped the spittle from his mouth with the back of his hand.

Sean remained unmoved by Ivan's impassioned speech. He couldn't care less. What he did know was that he would get that key away from the man. He leaned forward as if moved by his words.

"An Eire man? Yea, that would be something to see."

"Aye." Ivan's eyes widened. "You would have a place beside King Leofrid of England as one of his most trusted allies—if you help us. Why shouldn't more men from our fair isle be in powerful positions here as well?"

"I can think of no reason. And he has no doubt he can do this? This Leofrid? He is powerful enough now? Ten years later?"

Ivan hesitated. His eyes narrowing. Sean felt certain Ivan assessed whether the insult was intended or if he should overlook the comment.

"Yes. He is finally ready."

Sean stood, walking toward the man with an outstretched hand. His foot butted against the stake. His other leg stretched out the length of the chain. The insult was intentional. "I am behind him then. Together we will certainly win."

Ivan stood as well. "I knew you would join us when you understood our purpose."

This man was an idiot. "Of course. How could I not?"

Ivan moved in close and squatted down to insert the key into the solid lock securing the band at Sean's ankle. Sean glanced the way Ivan had come but saw no one. He smiled then reached down to wrap the chain around Ivan's neck. The man struggled against him, his small hands grabbing at the thick links held in Sean's iron grip as he tightened his hold. The gurgling sounds eventually stopped. Sean unwrapped the fetter and shoved the lifeless body away, retrieving the key from beneath Ivan. He wiggled it into the lock—

"Ye should probably stop there."

~

"Someone's coming."

Thomasina jumped at Niall's quiet voice beside her. She'd been transfixed by witnessing Sean's strength. His body fairly rippled with the powerful grip he'd had of the man, the chains manipulated as if they had weighed nothing. She took a slow, steadying breath. Without another word, Aldred and Lachlann jumped out from their hiding place to grab the body of the dead man and pull him into the woods. They dropped it beside her. His eyes, open and unseeing, bulged grotesquely. He stank. She clasped her hand over her nose and mouth and shifted to the side.

Sean's initial expression of confusion and defense had quickly changed to relief when Lachlann and Aldred disappeared back into the woods, hiding the evidence of what had transpired. He resumed his seat back on the ground, the key safely hidden and the chains and irons still attached.

A Norman soldier came from between the two huts with a bucket of water. He turned toward Sean without even glancing their way. When he offered him the wooden ladle, Sean tipped his head in thanks then drank with loud slurping noises. Upon further inspection, Thomasina noticed the area around his mouth appeared mottled and one of his eyes looked swollen shut. She turned to ask Niall about it but he quickly held his finger to his mouth for her to keep silent.

"How long until the messenger returns from York?" Sean asked, his mouth moved awkwardly and his words sounded garbled.

The soldier shrugged then dropped a crust of bread beside him. "Best eat. Keep your strength up."

Sean shoved the nourishment to his mouth. If he'd been tortured as badly as it looked, even the bread would be difficult for him to eat. She'd not thought of needing to care for him. She'd only thought of getting him back.

The four stayed hidden until the soldier returned to the main road. Lachlann was the first at Sean's side. He took the key and started working it into the lock. Aldred stood watch behind him for anyone else. Niall offered his own water skin to Sean who drank again. The bread in his hand was barely touched but soaked with blood where he'd had it to his mouth.

"Oh, Sean," Thomasina's voice broke. She tore off a tiny piece of bread, dropped some of the water on it and brought to his blistering lips.

He closed his eye and accepted the nourishment into his mouth then drank again.

"Ye're free." Lachlann patted his leg, helped him to stand, then wrapped an arm around his body to take his weight as Niall led the way back into the woods.

They paused over the body they'd hidden for Sean.

"My thanks for that." Sean shook his head then glanced between the other two men. "How long were ye here?"

"Long enough to hear his taunting," Niall spoke, his tone solemn. "They've sent no one to verify yer story."

"It appears not," Sean said. "The lying bastard."

"Oh, we ken Ivan," Lachlann said. "He deserved to die... many times over."

"After he'd been soundly beaten," Aldred smirked.

Niall looked back toward the now empty chains. "We'd best move quickly."

"Let us dump his body into the ocean!" Aldred said it as if he'd thought of a great game they could play. "The bastard's body will be tossed up against the rocks as it deserves."

Niall smiled back. "Yea. The beating he missed."

"Stay here." Lachlann settled Sean down then patted his leg in an affectionate gesture. Thomasina almost laughed at Sean's shocked expression at the display. "We'll be back anon."

Niall took the legs. Lachlann the arms. Aldred went ahead to see that the path was clear. They traveled through the cover of the forest then were out of sight.

Thomasina became aware of the suddenly awkward situation. Sean's eyes were closed. He seemed to be asleep. She reached toward the nasty looking swelling on the side of his head. His hand darted out to grab her wrist before she touched him.

"'Tis worse than it looks." He still didn't open his eyes.

She smirked. "How can ye ken that?"

"Yer concerned for me and ye need not be." His voice was flat.

Thomasina turned her gaze to her hand. He released it immediately. She turned back but his eyes remained closed.

"How are ye doing that?"

"I've been able to ken yer thoughts since we met."

She wasn't certain if his tone warmed or if it was her imagination but her heart raced at the statement. "What do ye mean 'ken my thoughts'?"

Sean started to take a deep breath but stopped, his grimace indicating the amount of pain he was in.

"Just sit still."

She pulled the bread from where she'd tucked it inside her tunic.

His eye flew open. "I do not want it."

She frowned. "But ye need yer nourishment to keep up yer strength."

He closed his eyes. "I told ye. Ye need not be concerned."

The three reappeared, minus one body, without a sound.

"Are ye able to travel Sean?" Lachlan questioned.

Sean stood with a wince that forced Thomasina to reach toward him. He turned on her. "Dunna even think about touching me."

Lachlann reached around his back and took Sean's weight again. He offered Thomasina a reassuring smile. "He meant he's too heavy for ye to help."

"Come with me and get the horses ready." Niall took her hand, Aldred following behind. She didn't feel right leaving Lachlann to deal with Sean and his broken body but her brother gave her no choice. He weaved his way through the trees to the horses.

"He is in a lot of pain." She stated the obvious. "Who beat him so mercilessly?"

Niall mounted his horse. "He'll tell us when he's ready."

He leaned down to bring her up behind him. Aldred mounted his horse but didn't follow.

"Where is he going?" Thomasina asked.

"To see to the sheep."

Niall and Thomasina traveled silently behind the buildings of the village, Lachlann's horse in tow. Lachlann helped Sean onto the horse.

"I must find Tadhg's knife," Sean said.

Lachlann and Niall exchanged glances but shook their heads. "He is not right in the mind."

"Tadhg is his kinsman. The knife was held until Daisy was returned."

"Roana." Sean's weakened voice could barely be heard.

She looked at him, longing for a glimpse of that exasperated expression. Nothing.

"Yes, Roana. Sean needs to get the knife back. We need to find it."

"The blacksmith's," Sean said.

Thomasina nibbled the inside of her lip. "Yea. We will find it."

"And Daisy." Sean sounded ready to pass out. He lurched to the side but Lachlann was there to hold him up.

"We need to get moving. When the soldiers find him gone, they'll come looking for him."

"Nae! He must have the knife!" Thomasina used her most demanding tone.

Niall searched her face but only nodded. "Take him up the hill. Tommy and I will catch up."

Lachlann managed to mount his horse. He wrapped Sean's arms around him and Thomasina would have laughed at the comical expression they both had if not for the seriousness of them getting caught. With a sure hold of Sean's clasped hands, Lachlann kicked the horse into a trot. They didn't have time to take an easy gait for Sean's comfort.

Niall and Thomasina ducked into the blacksmith's hut with the sunlight just making its presence known.

"So what does this knife look like?" Niall put his hands to his hips and glanced around the clutter.

Thomasina's stomach dropped. "I dunna ken."

Her brother's piercing gaze said it all. How could she have not asked Sean about the knife? She swept her hair out of her face. "'Tis a knife. How many knives can there be?" She spied the coffer and went to it. "It has to be here."

Thomasina picked up Sean's shield that leaned against the side. His brat and sack were all there.

"These are Sean's as well."

"I will put them round back."

Niall returned and they both knelt in front of the chest, poking around helmets, avoiding sharp blades, then started again. Top to bottom. Side to side.

"Damn. I see no knives."

Niall sat on the floor, leaning his back against the chest. "'Tis of such great importance?"

"Aye. 'Tis to him! That I ken for certain—he had to get the knife back." Irritation teased at her like a bug that wouldn't leave. "I did have my horse back after our loving father gave her away, but I had to wait until Sean retrieved his precious knife before he would part with her."

Niall frowned. "So Sean had Daisy?"

Thomasina glanced at her brother's expression and wished she'd just kept her mouth shut about the whole thing. "It matters little now."

A sudden alertness lit his eyes and he turned toward her. "So this man ye barely ken had yer horse?"

"This is immensely frustrating."

"And look who we found here!"

Niall and Thomasina turned as one to see the man staggering toward them. Their father. They stood, Niall taking her by the hand as if to give her support.

"Been looking for ye, son. Ye been off kissing the arse of my brother again?"

His slurred speech gave no doubt of his condition.

"Father. And why would ye be looking for me except ye're in need of my help?"

The smaller man shook his head and eyed his children. A critical assessment that ended with a scornful expression. "Ye two. Ye'll be the death of me."

Talking could be heard as people were approaching. Thomasina thought she recognized the voice of the blacksmith. She wished to be anywhere but here and squeezed Niall's hand. He returned the gesture without looking toward her but nodded his head.

When they were children and the slightest wrong thing could set their father off, they learned to communicate without words. If the hand was squeezed and the other person understood, they'd squeeze back. She swallowed down the fear threatening to overtake her. Niall was here now. He would take care of this.

The blacksmith entered talking with another man. Thomasina reeled back at the sight of the gray-haired man with the ruddy complexion.

Angus O'Reilly. When he looked at her, a smile of pleasure spread across his face. He stepped quickly toward her with an outstretched hand. Niall moved in front of her, cutting him off and stopping him from getting too close.

"What are ye about, boy? Step aside for Angus. He's betrothed to our little Thomasina."

Thomasina struggled to take a breath. Fear spread through her like a wildfire out of control.

"I'm not certain ye're remembering correctly," Niall's voice faltered.

The sounds around them became muffled.

Their father stomped toward them. He stood nose to chest with Niall, an angry scowl across his face. "Do ye think I'm daft? I ken who my daughter's betrothed to."

Angus stayed where he was as did his smile. "Hello, Tommy."

She shook her head. Niall squeezed her hand but didn't budge. An anchor in her maelstrom.

"So the lad is the bride you went to retrieve?" The blacksmith narrowed his eyes at her. "Aye, Angus, I have your horse and apparently your bride. Let me go get Roana."

Angus jerked his head toward the man. "Roana?"

Thomasina's heart skipped a beat. A muffled shout of alarm sounded in the distance.

"Nae. The horse is named Daisy." Angus turned back to her. "Tommy's horse."

She couldn't speak. Niall squeezed her hand again. She couldn't respond.

The blacksmith glanced at the man and shrugged. He continued out toward the back.

"She will be yers again when we're wed. How have ye been, Tommy? I've been searching for ye."

"Father!" Thomasina's voice sounded hoarse. "What are ye about?"

She looked him up and down, searching for the sack of coins that Sean had thrown at him. His bloodshot eyes revealed nothing. Not that he was lying. Not that he had seen her just the day before. Not that he knew anything other than what he was saying.

"I've married my precious daughter off to a good man." He stepped closer to Angus, wrapping an arm around the taller man's shoulder. "He'll treat ye right."

A few soldiers passed by outside. "The Norman slayer has escaped."

She squeezed Niall's hand again. He dropped his head.

The blacksmith stopped in the road at the front of his shop. "Fed and watered and good as new."

Angus turned to the horse and reached inside his pocket. Thomasina watched in horror as he pulled out the sack of coins that Sean had given to her father. He opened it, took out a coin, and passed to the blacksmith with a smile. "I thank ye."

"Did Father give ye the coins, then?" Thomasina kept her voice quiet. Fear was turning to rage.

"Aye. Quite a dowry ye come with." Angus shot her a quick smile.

"That's quite a feat considering—" Thomasina started.

"She no longer comes with a dowry." Niall faced the man and spoke in a strong voice. "My father was ostracized from our clan. He lost everything."

Angus' eyes narrowed. "What are ye saying?"

"Those are the coins to pay off my father's debt to ye."

"To hell with ye, boy! That's her dowry. Just as I said." Their father's brows slashed down in anger, his fist curling at his side. "Dunna be telling lies about us."

When their father moved to grab Thomasina's arm, Niall shoved him away.

"Ye're not touching her." He faced Angus' angry expression. "Nor are ye. She's betrothed to another."

"There's been no such agreement." Their father, barely able to keep from falling at his son's push, puffed his chest out and turned to the other man. "The boy's daft."

"'Tis a done deed," Niall said.

Silence fell over them like a blanket. Thomasina held her breath feeling as if she were facing a pack of wolves. One false move and they'd be jumping on her, ripping her apart. She glanced between the two of them and waited. More shouting outside. Her father scrunched up his face.

looking to be rummaging through his sodden brain to pick up any trace of the event actually happening. A long few minutes passed before he finally spoke.

"Ye've given up yer innocence then?"

"'Tis rightfully due her husband and no one else." Niall intercepted her having to answer. His avoidance of the question caused Thomasina's heart to soar. "Ye dunna debate the truth of that, do ye, father?"

Angus' face darkened with his fury. He stepped closer to Niall and when he would have grabbed at Thomasina, her brother stopped his hand short. He gripped the older man's wrist. His lips disappeared into a tight, thin line.

"Dunna be touching what's not yers." Niall's expression curled in a scornful scowl.

The man didn't speak at first. He looked to be measuring Niall's mettle. As if he could see inside his soul and learn if he was telling the truth. Thomasina prayed with all her might that he could not.

Angus glanced where Niall's hand held his arm. He ripped it from Niall's grip. Despite his advanced years, this man was quite strong. If he ever took hold of her in anger, there was no telling how she would survive.

"If ye're lying to me, *boy*, I'll find out. And I'll have her myself—once and for all."

Angus turned to Thomasina, leering at every inch of her most intimately before smiling. A wide smile that spoke of his long held desire to take her.

Her stomach clenched.

He turned back to Niall. "And I'll slice yer throat just for the hell of it."

The man snorted and turned toward their father. "Ye've not paid enough. Not nearly enough."

He stomped toward Daisy. The blacksmith backed away, allowing the other man to mount unassisted. Without a backward glance, Angus rode away.

Their father scratched his head. "Guess that's done with."

Niall was beside himself with anger. "What are ye playing at? Ye'd give him Thomasina? He's a defiler of women and children."

Their father's eyes seemed to focus on Niall. Intently. An expression Thomasina hadn't seen on him for quite some time. He stepped closer and tipped his head before he spoke. "*Were* ye lying?"

Nae!" Niall answered without hesitation, his tone adamant.

Their father's eyes held his. She couldn't be certain but he looked as if he'd noticed something in Niall's tone. Niall had sounded a bit too... forceful. Thomasina swallowed. For the smallest second, she feared he was about to call Angus back and tell him it was all a lie. Then their father stepped back, his hands dropping to his sides.

Niall kneeled down and picked up something from the ground. He took Thomasina's hand and led her out to his horse around back. Their father watched but said nothing.

Once mounted, they headed away from the village, following the narrow path that led to the top of the rise where the cave was. Neither spoke.

CHAPTER 12

The pain in Sean's side finally lessened and he had slept on and off for a short while. His limbs were stiff and painful when he tried to move them.

"Drink this."

It was Lachlann that was beside him every time he opened his eyes. Lachlann nursed him along, giving him water and broth, and some sort of foul smelling tea to ease his pains. Sean wanted to ask about Thomasina but he knew better than that. Neither she nor Niall seemed to be nearby.

"Is there much pain?"

Sean shook his head but the pounding across his skull kept his movements to a minimum.

"Methinks ye're lying through yer teeth, old man."

The desire to laugh was there but he knew it would be painful. He offered a smile.

"There ye go. See, now I'm believing ye." Lachlann rolled his eyes before walking back to the small fire.

The cave was cozy with the fire. A peaceful place. A quiet place where Sean could think. He'd come close to the end of his life and his biggest regret? Spending so much of his time chasing after someone who didn't want him. He wasn't going to make that mistake again. Once he was strong enough, he'd get back to Eire. Certainly getting there the way he'd come was no longer an option. No doubt he was a hunted man.

"My thanks for hiding me." Sean's voice sounded weak. He coughed to clear his throat. "Where are the sheep?"

"Aldred took care of them."

Sean nodded. "I don't mean to put ye in harm's way."

Lachlann stood beside him. "Dunna fash yerself. If not for ye being a fellow warrior, I'd have to be seeing to ye for the sweet lass Thomasina anyway."

Sean struggled to sit up but Lachlann urged him down. "Now. Ye're not ready for that. I dinna mean to upset ye."

"Thomasina cares little for me."

"Ah, spoken like a man who's had his heart broken a time or two."

"Yea. Once was quite enough."

Lachlann turned to him and searched his face. "Ye're starting to look human again. That's good. We dunna want to be scaring the lass with yer face all purpled and swollen."

"Enough! She would not care. She's no different than Brighit."

"Brighit? Of the MacNaughton Clan?"

Sean's weakened body became instantly alert and pain shot through him as his muscles stiffened. "Yea. The same. Do ye ken her?"

Lachlann laughed. "Aye. She's a bonny fox, that one. I had the pleasure of seeing her to the Priory." He looked over at Sean. "She's the ripest fruit I've ever laid eyes on."

Sean smiled. He couldn't take offense. It was true. And Sean, the arse, had been trying to pick that fruit forever. "Yea, but she's wed another."

"Peter? Did she wed him? That doesna surprise me. The man would lay down his life for her. She will be well taken care of by him, dunna ye worry."

Sean thought about that. It was a blessing to know she would spend her days protected and well-loved. It came as a surprise that the fact was suddenly enough for him. He realized he wanted her happy. He really hadn't wanted her for the right reasons. "She was quite happy with him as her husband. Already carrying his bairn."

Lachlann smiled. "She never seemed like the nun-type to me. Too impassioned. Ye ken?"

Yes, he'd sensed it, too. He seemed to have quite an ability for seeing beneath the surface. With Thomasina, even more so. He'd enflamed her passion. But it wasn't to be. Not when the fate of a clan rested on the outcome.

"Ye need to eat. The fish jump out of the loch here."

"Yea." Sean smiled again. His face less stiff. "I dinna mind Thomasina thinking it was my great prowess that caught the fish. She hates to see the skinning of the bloody animals."

Lachlann glanced at him. "Is that how 'tis with her?"

"Yea. I dunna wish to make the lass uncomfortable."

Lachlann continued to look at him. "Are not most women squeamish about such things?"

Sean shrugged. He had never noticed. "The fish smells good. Mayhap I'm getting my strength back."

"I truly hope so."

Lachlann looked to the opening of the cave. Sean followed his gaze. Niall and Thomasina stood in the entrance. She looked exhausted and Sean's arms ached to hold her. He kept himself rigid, his face expressionless.

"There has been some trouble." It was Niall who finally spoke.

"What is amiss?" Lachlann came to Sean, bending down to help him sit up when he struggled. "Has it to do with Sean?"

"He is a wanted man. They search for him, calling him the Norman slayer." Niall paused. "We ran into our father."

Thomasina looked away and Niall closed the distance to the other men. "O'Reilly tried to take her away while I stood right there."

Sean leaned forward, ignoring the pain coursing through him. "If he touched her, I will run him through."

Niall reached an arm to Sean to help him stand. "He will not get near her. Not while I'm alive."

"But that bastard—our father—had given him yer coins as my dowry," Thomasina finally spoke up.

Sean's face paled. Everyone lurched toward him before he crumbled to the ground. They sat him slowly back down.

"Ye need to take care, man, ye've had a bad beating," Niall said.

Sean's eyes closed, the sounds around were muffled as he struggled to stop the room from spinning. "Water, please."

Thomasina took the water from Lachlann's hand and held it to Sean's lips.

"My thanks, Lachlann." He opened his eyes to Thomasina but didn't speak.

Her face heated and she moved away.

Lachlann touched her hand when he took the skin. "He's had nothing but my ugly face to look at while ye've been gone."

Sean lay back down and draped his arm over his face. "Tell me."

Niall sat down beside the man. "My father gave O'Reilly the coins and told him it was Thomasina's dowry. There had been no discussion it was payment for his debts."

Sean fisted his hand and smashed it against the ground. "I dunna like just laying here when I want to kick the man's arse."

"I told them she was betrothed."

Sean lowered his arm and turned to face Tommy's brother. His expression gave no indication of what he was planning.

Thomasina brought the skin to Sean again. "Ye need to drink."

Her lovely, green eyes were wide, beseeching him to accept the water from her. He opened his mouth for her ministrations.

She nodded and smiled. "It smells of fish. I'll get ye some."

Sean watched her as she walked away. Lachlann was quick to step up and help her. While the two were talking, Niall moved a bit closer.

"So we have a bit of a problem." Niall turned to face him, his voice quiet. "We need to get her married—now. I dunna trust O'Reilly or my father."

"So ye need to get to yer uncle and make the match ye spoke of." The ache in his chest as he spoke the words felt nearly as intense as the pain in his body. He didn't want to see her married to another, but it wasn't his choice. "I understand ye leaving me here. Getting her safely away is more urgent now."

Especially since Sean was a hunted man. Her being near him put her in danger. He would not have it. She needed to be protected and away from him.

"Nae. We will not just leave ye here."

"The Normans are hunting me down! Ye need to leave me here."

"They will not come this way till the morrow. We have time to get ye to the coast and to another boat to take ye home." He placed his hand on Sean's shoulder. "Ye're a good man for seeing after Tommy."

Niall accepted the fish Lachlann handed to him.

"A few miles north, there's a little village of fishermen," Lachlann said. "There must be a handy boatmen willing to see ye across."

Thomasina scooted her bottom close to Sean. He wanted to wrap his arm around her. Pull her closer. She leaned over a bit, a small piece of fish in her fingers. Her eyes sparkled and he stared into their depths. She was intent on watching that the fish made it to his mouth. He was intent on feeling her close the distance between them. The scent of her skin. The feel of her hand where it rested lightly on his chest. He took the food, his lips closing around her fingers.

Thomasina took a shaky breath, finally tearing her eyes from his mouth. She stared back at him, his eyes unwavering on her. Her lips parted and she smiled but it was a half-hearted smile. Melancholy.

"My thanks."

Niall cleared his throat and stood abruptly. His expression tight with disapproval. "Methinks he may be able to feed himself, Tom. What say ye, Lachlann? Is he up for it?"

"I've never known eating fish to be a very taxing endeavor. Let us sit ye up a little more. Slowly so ye dunna pass out again. That's probably far enough."

The four ate in silence. Then Lachlann went about picking up the few things they'd taken out of their bags and put them back in preparation for leaving.

Niall blew a loud breath, his hands resting on his hips. "Well, there's still a few hours of daylight left. We'd best get started if ye're up to it."

"Yea." Sean nodded, sitting up a little more. The room didn't shift around him. "I'm certain I can ride."

Lachlann helped him up. "Perhaps sitting up by the fire for a few minutes while yer food settles?"

"Nae! Thomasina is not safe here."

"He's right. We need to leave this place."

Riding as before, they headed north. When it was too dark to travel, they set up camp nestled in a small clearing with steep cliffs on three sides. It would be difficult for the Normans or even their father to find them here.

Sean's body ached and he accepted the coverings offered. He was quickly asleep.

Thomasina lay beside her brother, sharing the same blanket, and watched the sun as it slowly lightened the night sky.

"Are ye asleep?" Niall's voice was quiet and he rolled toward her.

"Nae. I've been waiting for the sunrise. 'Tis bitter cold here. I pray Sean is warm enough."

"Ye care for the man?"

"Yea. He's a good man."

He took her hand, rubbing it between his own to help ward off the cold. "I've not slept much either. I fear what O'Reilly will do. I've all but told him ye've given up yer innocence to yer husband. I lied."

"And we parted ways with him."

"Yea. 'Tis all fine unless he decides to come after us."

She turned on her side to face him. "Ye think he may do that?"

"He was mad as the devil at losing ye."

Thomasina shivered and it wasn't from the cold. "But ye told him I was a virgin no longer."

"And he may think on it and decide I was lying. Father knew I was lying."

"Do ye believe he would tell O'Reilly?"

Niall shrugged, rolled onto his back, and looked heavenward. "The man is a drunken fool."

They watched the flight of a lark as it filled the air with the first songs of the new day.

Niall turned his head toward her, his gaze intense. "If ye've feelings for the warrior, tell me now."

The fluttering began again, her pulse racing to keep up. "Methinks ye ken."

"It would be safest to see ye wed to him now. That way, if O'Reilly finds us, there will be no question. He will not want ye if ye've been with another. 'Tis yer innocence he craves."

A shiver of repulsion tripped up her backbone. O'Reilly had lusted after her even when she was a child? If not for her brother and his friend's protection, the man could easily have forced himself on her, ripped her asunder even, to accommodate his perverse desires. Nothing would be worse than having him touch her.

"I ken how much ye've done to get back into the clan. I want ye to be welcomed back in as yer own man and stop this solitary life. I am not so selfish to think of only myself."

"I ken that. Since our own father's a drunk, 'tis up to me as yer brother to see to yer betrothal. If O'Reilly gets his hands on ye, it'll be too late to make a better choice for ye." He cupped her cheek. The warmth from his hand calmed her. "Methinks the warrior will be kind to ye. I canna say the same about any clans our uncle may choose to ally with. This may be what is best for ye."

"Yea. If he is willing to take me to wife."

"How could he not be?" He pulled her in close for a hug. "I'll speak with him."

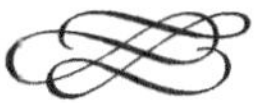

Sean's body screamed with every movement but he refused to show his weakness. He wouldn't allow them to waste any more time getting Thomasina safely away. The coast was just beyond them, the salt air already surrounding them. He'd find a boat and be home by nightfall. With the weight of his heart heavy in his chest, he mounted the horse behind Lachlann.

Thomasina reached up to him, a water skin near to bursting in her hand. "Ye need to remember to drink."

Sean nodded. "Thank ye."

Niall offered his arm to her and she jumped up behind him as she had with Sean. She turned to him and smiled. His heart squeezed.

"Where did ye learn such a thing as that?" Niall's amazement came through in his voice.

She dipped her chin. "I've been practicing."

"Let us hope ye'll soon not be needing the trews. Once properly dressed as a lass, that will be a bit more difficult," Niall offered and urged his horse to lead.

Lachlann stayed to the right, following close. Sean glimpsed over the man's shoulder at Thomasina's fine backside. He would have enjoyed seeing her in a dress, dipped in at her narrow waist, molding to her womanly form, her hair spreading out around her. He sighed.

"What is amiss?"

Sean hadn't realized he'd sighed out loud. "Just thinking of my many regrets."

Lachlann slowed his horse and fell back a bit. "Have ye many?"

"Yea. The threat of the beheading brought many quickly to mind. More than I'd care to admit."

"Any ye can turn around and rectify to yer liking?"

Sean wanted to wed Thomasina. It had felt right to call her his betrothed. His chest tightened. He wanted her with him. He couldn't imagine himself continuing on in the boat without her. He would miss everything about her. Her smile. Her sparkling, green eyes. Her angry frowns. Her determination.

He cleared his throat. "I am afeared not. 'Tis not to be."

"Have ye given it all ye have in ye? Like in battle? Like it were a matter of life and death?"

Life without Thomasina did not seem like much of a life. "'Tis not a simple thing."

Lachlann stopped the horse and turned his head to speak over his shoulder. "Are ye certain, Sean? Can ye leave the love of yer life behind on the shore when ye get into that boat? Without ever knowing how she fares? Without being the one to see to protecting her?" He glanced at him. "Without being the one to see to her happiness? Knowing that ye're the one who would lay down yer life for her?"

"I am a hunted man. They could kill me and she would be left with no one to protect her." It was hard to breathe. "And we both know the clan must come first."

Lachlann nodded.

Up ahead, Niall stopped and turned toward them, a frown on his face. "What is amiss?"

"Methinks the lass deserves some happiness," Lachlann continued in his low voice.

Thomasina looked around her brother. A small smile on her lips. Her eyes fixed on Sean.

Could he really just walk away from her and this chance for happiness?

"We're settled." Lachlann's voice was louder. "Stone in my shoe."

They were quickly behind Niall who continued to the edge of the trees. The sea strand beyond. The water a deep blue with little puffs of white here and there, as far as the eye could see.

"Yea." Sean spoke the single word aloud and his spirits rose. He knew what he had to do. He would ask Niall if he could take her to wife. He would tell him how deeply he cared for her. How he would spend the rest of his life seeing to her happiness.

The sound of voices drifted to them. Shouting. Niall pulled his horse up short just at the tree line. The words were indistinct, drowned out by the surf. Normans on foot rounded the sand dune to their left, headed toward them. They backed the horses further into the trees to remain hidden.

"What do ye think they are about?" Thomasina's fear could be heard in her voice.

Niall patted her hand where it wrapped around his waist. "They are soldiers. I dunna ken why they would be here."

Mounted soldiers came into view, passing the men on foot as they galloped along the water's edge.

"If we find no sign of him, we will look again." The man speaking wore mail. A mace, pole axe, and sword attached to his horse, readily at hand. "He will be wanting to head back to Eire like the weasel that he is."

Thomasina gasped. "They hunt for Sean!"

"We will loop around and come to shore further north," Niall said.

Even as he spoke dark shadows came from their right. They had the entire beach covered.

Lachlann backed up his horse until he could safely turn around.

Niall did the same, taking the lead. "Up to the loch."

Without another word, they wove their way through the trees and away from the coast. They encountered no other soldier. By midday, Niall led them into a gully with deep sides where the water ran fresh and bracken grew along the sides. They dismounted, leading the horses to the stream.

Niall paced. His expression livid. "I canna believe they come this far north."

Sean went down on one knee beside the water, cupping it in his hand for a drink. Guilt made it hard to swallow. They were hunting him down, putting the others in danger now. Putting Thomasina in danger.

"They believe I killed one of their own. The price on my head alone for each soldier killed would make it worth their while to hunt me down."

Niall stopped a few feet from him. His nostrils flaring in his indignation. Sean shoved down his own wants and settled his mind.

"Ye need to continue north without me. Go to yer uncle's clan," Sean said. "Thomasina needs to be wed."

"Nae!" Thomasina's face paled. "I will not leave ye here unprotected."

Sean smiled. "I am never unprotected, Thomasina. I'm a warrior."

"Yea. I ken that just fine."

Something about her tone gave him pause. "Yea?"

She rubbed her hands together then gave him a sideways glance. "Ye are a warrior first. Like when ye killed the soldier at the inn."

"Ye killed a soldier?" Niall's voice was higher than usual, loud and accusing. "Why did ye not tell us that?"

"He held a knife to yer sister's throat." Sean stood, keeping his eyes on her.

"So were ye a part of the slaughter or nae?"

Sean turned to the man. His expression stone cold. "Nae. I would take no part in the slaughtering of unarmed men. I fight to protect me and mine."

"Did he ken I was a woman?"

Sean's chest tightened at the memory. All around him forgotten but her, he remembered the intense need to save her. "I dunna ken for certain if he thought you a lass or a lad. When he moved to grab yer arse, he had to die."

"Tell me how *ye* knew I was a lass. My effeminacies?"

"Ye behave like a woman in many ways but ye fooled the others at the inn."

"Did I?"

Lachlann moved next to Niall.

"I canna follow."

"Methinks they need a moment," Lachlann said and led him a short distance away.

"So when ye killed him, were ye protecting ye or yers?"

Sean offered a quiet smile. "He offered no threat to *my* person."

"Ye or yers?" Thomasina repeated her question in a small voice.

"Ye spoke like a fighter yerself and I dinna want to see ye knocked on yer arse—fine as it was." Sean's voice was hushed. He closed the distance between them. He needed to tell her how he felt, especially if he had to leave her behind. "Not while I was there beside ye."

A glistening of moisture appeared on her eyelids. His breath caught in his chest. Without thinking twice he leaned down to cup her cheek and drew her in closer. He kissed her lips with the lightest pressure before pulling back slightly. "I considered ye mine. From the first."

Her eyes rounded. "I liked to be yers."

"Dunna make this any harder than 'tis. Ye're ripping my heart out."

Sean wanted to kiss her again. It didn't matter what he wanted. Not anymore.

She licked her lips and glanced at his mouth then back to his eyes. "Kiss me like I'm yers. Just once more."

He closed his eyes and shut out everything around them. He closed his eyes to feel every tender sensation. He closed his eyes to etch the feel of her on his heart. The kiss was tender at first. Tasting. Remembering. Mourning. When she shifted closer, his arms wrapped around her. He held her against him, where she belonged, and memorized the feel of her in his arms. Her mouth became more insistent, opening for his tongue to plunder its depths. He groaned and pulled back.

"Nae, Thomasina. This canna be for us."

"How can I just say goodbye to ye? I dunna want to say goodbye. I want to stay with ye. Dunna ye want that?"

"More than anything in this world."

"If Lachlann had not come in, ye'd have made love to me." She whispered the words in the small space between their lips.

Sean took a shaky breath then crushed her against him. "'Tis all for the best." The words he was saying made no sense even to him. "Ye'll live up north with someone better suited to ye."

"Ye're suited to me."

"I hear I'm a brute."

Her laughter made her stomach move against him. He began to laugh as well. "Sorry I am that I said that."

"I was being hard on ye."

"But ye were right. I kept forgetting to behave like a boy. I think..." She pulled farther away creating a space between their bodies. "I think even then I wanted ye to see me as a woman."

"Aye, I could see ye just fine."

Niall cleared his throat. Sean pulled back, his face flushing with heat. He should not have given in to foolish desires. It only made it worse. Thomasina touched her finger to her lips, avoiding her brother's eyes.

Niall glanced between the two, a hard expression. "I believe we have some things to discuss."

Thomasina faced her brother, her hand on her hip. "Dunna be taking it out on him. I wanted him to kiss me. I *made* him kiss me."

The four stood silently then Lachlann started to laugh. Niall quickly joined in and then Sean.

Thomasina's jaw dropped. "Why are ye laughing?"

"A truly ridiculous thing to say," Niall said.

"Ye could not make him kiss ye if ye tried."

She gave an exasperated sigh then walked as far as the horses. "Ye're all brainsick."

"Tommy and I will see to the horses." Lachlann patted Niall's shoulder and added in a quiet voice. "Ye two talk."

Reality gripped Sean's throat. He could not swallow. "We were saying our goodbyes. I'm sorry I let it happen. I ken 'tis not right with her being intended for another."

"I think we need to talk about that."

Sean faced the stream, stiff backed. "Yea."

"She needs to be married."

"Yea. And what do ye need me to do?" He faced Niall.

"Marry the lass."

Sean's chest tightened at the words. "I thought I was not up to yer choosing."

He could hear the bitterness in his own voice.

"She is in love with ye."

"It is what is best for her that is important."

Niall shook his head, a look of disbelief etched across his face. "Do ye hear yerself?"

"Yea. I hear myself fine. I ken ye need to do what is best for the clan and it will be what is best for her."

"She does not care about the clan. I am the one who cares about the clan. Thomasina? She cares about ye."

Sean glanced toward her, his voice quiet. "And I care about her." He turned his intense gaze on Thomasina's brother. "I canna love her only part way, just enough to get her away from yer father. I need to love her all the way. I need her to go back with me to Eire. I need her by my side. Can ye give her up to me?"

Niall shifted his jaw, perhaps struggling with emotions. "I love my sister. I have looked out for her my whole life. Lachlann, Aldred, and I. We protected her always. I would not let her go with anyone who would offer any less. Yea. I can give her to ye, Sean."

The spark leapt into a flame. "I will protect her with my life."

"I ken ye will," Niall smirked. "It is best for her. Ye can protect her now. She's vulnerable otherwise. As 'tis now, my father and O'Reilly could take her."

Sean's jaw clenched. "She will come willingly to me as my wife or I'll not marry her. I care too much for her to take her against her will because ye've arranged it for her."

Niall nodded, his eyes narrowing as if trying to see into his thoughts. Sean looked away. He had said his peace. Now it was up to Niall.

"I do not see that as a problem." He pursed his lips together. "Do ye?"

Niall didn't wait for his answer but extended his hand. Sean accepted the gesture.

"It is not to where we have been living. Ye have until we arrive to assure yerself of her feelings for ye. Then we sign the contract. Lachlann and I will head west and keep an eye on the Normans." He faced Sean. "We will be back in the morning and we can plan our strategy."

Sean paused to consider what he was offering him. Consummation so no one could gainsay his rights as her husband. In his heart, he had meant what he told her. She was his from the first.

CHAPTER 14

$\mathcal{N}$iall walked to the horses where Lachlann and Thomasina waited, Sean close behind.

"We head to the house, Thomasina." Niall mounted his horse and reached toward his sister.

Sean intercepted his hand on Thomasina's arm. "Nae. She goes with me."

Her green eyes widened. "Are ye strong enough?"

"Yea." He took her hand and led her to the other horse.

Lachlann mounted behind Niall, a big smile on his face. "I'm going to miss ye, Sean," Lachlann batted his eyes as he spoke in a high, girly voice, "and yer strapping arms about my waist."

Sean kept a straight face. "I canna say the same."

He mounted and reached down to Thomasina, pulling her in front of him. She glanced toward her brother as if expecting an objection. Niall turned away and guided his horse northward, leaving them to follow.

She ducked her head, averting Sean's gaze. "Let me ken if I am too much for ye."

Sean offered a smile despite his body screaming out in pain. "Ye will never be too much for me."

Niall kept the horses at a slow pace no doubt to accommodate Sean's broken body. The scent of the woman in his arms was a balm to his bruises. She sat away from him, as if afraid to hurt him.

"Ye and yer brother are close?"

"Yea. He has always looked out for me." She faced front, her body stiffening. "After our mother died, our father began to drink. Soon he was always drunk. After we were sent away from the clan, Lachlann and Aldred would come and help my brother to provide for us."

"So they remain with the clan?"

"Yea. They come around more when the work for the harvest or the hunting is done with."

"Does yer uncle ken what they are doing?"

"Yea. I think he cares for us still and wants to ken that Niall and I are taken care of. 'Tis my father he opposed."

Sean wrapped an arm about her, pulling her in close. She sighed and relaxed against him.

"I would have gladly taken ye to wife after yer father left ye. I dunna want to do anything against yer clan."

Her shoulders stiffened.

"Being without a clan is a dangerous way for a man to live," Sean said.

She nodded against his chest.

"Will yer brother find a way into the clan if I take ye with me?"

Pulling away to face him, her eyes rounded. "I dunna ken about the clan."

He looked into the expressive green eyes that were intently measuring everything he said. "I want ye as my wife."

She wrapped her arms about his middle gently, as if she could somehow break him. "I dunna want to be left behind without ye."

He pulled back on the reins and wrapped her in his arms. She belonged there. He had no doubt about that. All his aches were forgotten with her there.

The touch of his lips on the top of Thomasina's head was such a simple gesture but it endeared him to her even more. He was a strong warrior, her Sean. She felt safe there in his arms. If she was the only way Niall could return to the clan, was it wrong for her to go with Sean? Was she condemning her brother to a solitary life?

Thomasina yearned to pull Sean closer, to hear his heartbeat but this was enough. To be surrounded by his strength. Encircled by his arms. Enclosed in his scent.

"I dunna ken if I can leave ye behind, Thomasina."

His words were spoken in a deep voice. A voice filled with emotion. A voice of longing.

"I dunna ken if I can stay behind without ye."

Sean exhaled on a long sigh almost as if he'd been holding his breath.

"Yer brother is a good man. He does not deserve to be ostracized because of yer father's failings." He tipped her chin up so he could see into her eyes. "I want ye by my side, Thomasina. Can ye take me as yer husband?"

The butterflies in her stomach soared into her chest. She reached up and kissed him. "Yea. I'll take ye as my husband."

Sean searched her face for something she didn't understand. "Do you ken what that means?"

She frowned but nodded. "Yea."

"It means I see to yer protection. Ye go where I go. Yer brother will nae longer have a say."

Thomasina looked away. Her brother had always been her protector. She abided by his wishes. If she had to choose, there was no choice at all. She would follow her husband. A shiver of anticipation emanated from her gut. Turning toward Sean, she schooled her features. "I want ye as my husband, Sean."

Sean crushed her to him with more strength than she would believe he held in his battered condition.

"Ye'll not regret it. I promise ye."

His words warmed her heart. With his lips touching her hair, his breath against her ear sent little waves of desire washing over her. He tipped her chin up to him and took her mouth. The kiss was a passionate sealing of their fates and his promise of what she would always mean to him.

Sean pulled away and smiled. Facing front, an arm still holding her against him, Sean urged the horse forward to catch up with Niall and Lachlann. Thomasina tightened her hold of him to keep from shifting away.

"How far to yer home?" Sean spoke without taking his eyes off the path.

Lachlann and Niall came into view.

"Just a few miles more."

"Will we be there before dark?"

"Yea."

He looked at her. "Hold tight."

Sean raced the horse past Niall and Lachlann.

"Which way?" he asked.

Trepidation tripped up Thomasina's spine at the speed he was traveling. She hugged him close. There would be no wedding night if he broke his neck falling from the horse.

"Just ahead. Mayhap ye should slow down a bit?"

She pointed to the round building off to the right. The trees hid it well. Sean slowed the horse to a stop and jumped down. He reached up to help her off. She slid down in front of him. His smile reached his eyes as he held her there against his body.

"Even my aches and pains are at bay with ye in my arms."

Breathless, she closed her eyes feeling overwhelmed at the sudden change in him. She shivered. He stilled.

"Dunna be afraid of me, Thomasina." His large hand gently held her head against his chest. His words resonating through his body. "I'll never allow ye to be hurt by anyone. Not even me."

Niall and Lachlann came up behind.

"It looks as if we have a joining to see to." Niall smiled at his sister. "I take it ye've agreed to marry the man and put him out of his misery?"

"Yea." She pulled away and straightened her clothing.

"Good thing. The man was pining for ye something fierce." Lachlann nodded his head as if assessing something's worth. "Ye'll be good together."

"And what of Niall?" Thomasina wished she had not spoken the words as soon as they were out.

Sean held her close to his side. The tension in his body increased.

Niall jerked around to face her. "I will be fine. Dunna be worrying about me, little sister."

"Aldred and me will lo—" Lachlann said.

"—be a royal pain in my arse as always. I will have my hands quite full. Ye'll barely be missed."

He cleared his throat and headed through the opening of the sad, little hut with clumps of missing thatch and a crooked door that did not shut all the way. Sean took her hand, keeping her back while the other two went inside.

"What is amiss?" she asked.

He pulled her close, behind the horses so that they were partially hidden from the others. His breath warm against her cheek. "I want to ken yer mine. I dunna want to wait." His lips were firm against hers, persistent. Her body immediately responded. He pulled her in closer as if sensing it, his hands roaming her back to slide over her backside. He moaned into her mouth where his tongue sparred against her own.

"Thomasina?" Niall called from the doorway.

Sean released her, a smile on his face. "I'm here." She called and smiled back.

"Are ye coming in?"

Sean gave her a quick kiss.

"I am seeing to my bag," Sean spoke to her then answered in a louder voice, "we are coming anon."

He untied the bag and opened it. She recognized the items from her earlier rummaging. When he pulled out the vellum, he paused. "I dinna ken this was meant for ye when I had it written but I offer it to ye with my whole heart, Thomasina."

"What is it?"

"A marriage contract."

CHAPTER 15

Sean took her hand and led her toward the house. Her grip tightened as they moved closer to the entrance. Her wide eyes spoke of the memories assailing her. The fear gripping her. He needed to re-focus her thoughts.

"Ye and yer brother were happy here sometimes?"

She turned to him as if she'd forgotten he was there then smiled. "Yea. We were. Sometimes."

It was a small, one room building, dark and smelling of sheep and mold. Thomasina immediately saw to taking care of the rushes. Niall worked on starting a fire in the open hearth at the rear. Lachlann lit the candle on the trestle table centered in the middle of the room then went to the wooden plank partially hidden beneath. He lifted it up, revealing a hollowed out area in the earthen floor. First he withdrew a covered clay crock then a large, cloth-encased hunk of cheese and replaced the wooden door.

"I'm starving." He broke off a piece of the cheese, popped it into his mouth, and turned to face Sean. "Do ye need a wedding feast?"

"It may be nice but not necessary. Unless Thomasina prefers it." He spoke the words as she returned with thick, winter grass that she tossed about the floor to cover the hard-packed dirt.

"A feast?" Thomasina shrugged. "Any food would be a feast to me. I'm starving."

She went to the trestle table and opened the crock. She smelled it. "I put these up just a bit ago. They smell good."

With two hands she carried the container to the fire and placed it close to the flame. "This will be good for tonight. Dunna eat all the cheese, Lachlann."

He stopped chewing when all eyes were on him. "I will not." He had trouble saying the words with his mouth full.

Thomasina glanced around before heading toward an area Sean had not noticed. A thick tapestry hung from the wood beam, closing it off from the rest of the room. She secured the heavy material to one side with a cord. The space was barely large enough to stand in with the pallet and a small chest. Sean's heart squeezed seeing the small area she had for her own and her meager belongings. Thomasina deserved so much more.

She kneeled in front of the chest and lifted the top of the coffer. With great reverence, she began to pull out what appeared to be a gown. She turned suddenly toward him, dropping the material and stood. "I need but a moment."

Pulling the hanging back into place, she enclosed herself within. Sean glanced at the other two who were watching him.

"Methinks she prepares herself for ye." Niall said. "And I believe we have some business to attend to."

"Yea." Sean slipped the tie off the contract and unrolled it on top of the table. Lachlann and Niall moved in close. "This is what I bring to the marriage."

The other two read the neatly written words conveying Sean's worth and worldly holdings which he offered to his wife at their joining. Once finished, they exchanged glances and stood up as one.

Sean helped himself to the jug of mead set back on the shelf behind the trestle. "Shall we have a drink before signing?"

Niall moved in close, glancing toward where Thomasina was still ensconced. "I had no idea of yer wealth. Are ye cer—"

"Dunna say it." Sean's tone was sharp but to put a price on his feelings for Thomasina would not be done. "I had this written up with the intention of marrying a woman whom I had no true love for. An infatuation. The feelings I have for yer sister come from deep in my heart. It runs like blood in my veins. Dunna say Thomasina is not of equal value to me. Her value surpasses all that I have—Nae, all that I could ever hope to attain in this lifetime. Her worth is beyond measure and that she is willing to take me and give me the honor of having her to wife is worth more than all the gold in the world to me. Dunna speak of this to her, I beg ye."

Niall nodded, a somber expression. "I see no reason to discuss it further." He took the quill and ink tucked in the far corner to add his signature before handing it to Sean.

The intensity of emotion threatened to overwhelm Sean. He swallowed and tried not to burst out into song or smile like a fool. Bending his head, he made his signature in strong, bold letters. He exhaled.

"May God also add his blessing to this union," Niall said. He held the jug up in the air. "Let us drink."

Each man took a hefty swallow. A movement in the corner caught Sean's eye. A vision he had longed to see. Thomasina stood dressed in a light blue gown that hugged every womanly curve, her brushed auburn hair cascading around her shoulders fell past her hips. Her eyes were downcast, her unease more than apparent as she waited for a response. He walked to her, stopping at arm's length.

"Thomasina, ye are as beautiful as I imagined ye to be."

She tipped her head up, a smile lighting up her face. Her green eyes sparkled in the firelight. "Ye imagined me?"

"Yea."

"In a dress?"

"Yea, every way. While awake and asleep." He glided one hand down her hair, pausing to rub a wavy lock between his fingers to feel its silkiness. "I never imagined yer hair quite so soft."

She turned a pretty shade of pink. Niall stepped up to take her hand and brought her to stand in front of the trestle. Sean came up beside her, not daring to touch her for fear he wouldn't be able to stop. He'd imagined she would be a beautiful lass but the real thing was a bit like getting a fist to the gut and the wind knocked out of you. If he'd have seen her at some gathering, he'd have been drawn to her. That certainty encouraged him.

When she glanced toward him, he could see her nerves threatening to get the better of her. He smiled. A smile meant to ease any fears. A smile meant to show he had no doubts. A smile meant to convey his intense pleasure at marrying her.

Niall took the place on the opposite side of the table. "Well, I take the position as head of the family since our father is a drunkard. Does anyone object?"

Heads nodded in agreement.

"Then let it be so." Niall cleared his throat, his voice suddenly sounding tight. "I find this man, Sean of the MacNaughton Clan, a good man with much to offer to my only sister including home, protection, and the promise of children."

"I accept this man's offer of marriage and willingly agree to this contract where we have both affixed our names but I take *yer* desires to heart, Thomasina. Do ye find him acceptable as one ye can cleave unto as the scriptures ordain?"

All turned to Thomasina. Her wide eyes and raised brows assured Sean that this was not the normal route her clan took to marriage. Her face lighting up convinced him she was more than pleased to have her say. "Yea. I find him acceptable as my husband."

He directed himself to Sean. "Do ye offer her yer love and promise to take none other and do ye vow to care for her as yer own body?"

"Yea."

He turned to Thomasina. "Do ye offer him yer respect even when ye're mad as hell? And agree to not withhold yerself from him?"

"Yea."

Niall placed a long length of silken ribbon along the table. "Place yer hands together."

Sean and Thomasina flattened their palms together.

Niall tied the ribbon as one around their wrists then continued wrapping. "With the tying of this ribbon, like the joining of yer lives, may yer strength be measured no longer as two but as one. For as two have joined together as one, having the blessing of our Lord, no man may break the tie that binds."

He ended with a small bow atop their fingers. "And as the kiss symbolizes the acceptance of this unbreakable bond, Sean, ye may kiss yer wife and Tom—Thomasina, ye may kiss yer husband."

Lachlann cheered and Niall joined in, slapping each other on the back as if they'd accomplished a great feat. Sean leaned in toward her, their bound hands a slight hindrance to the embrace. When she tipped her head up for his kiss, he felt suddenly shy and hesitated. He searched her lovely face to remember forever. This was where he belonged. This was the woman intended for him. This was where his happily ever after would be found.

He became overwhelmed with the need to tell her how he felt. Quite a revelation for the man who does not share how he feels. But with Niall and Lachlann watching them, this was not the time. He set it aside. Tonight would be soon enough to admit his feelings to her. He touched his lips to hers, savoring her taste, her smell, her timid response.

"A drink!" Lachlann held up the jug.

Thomasina tensed. A glance at her confirmed she preferred to not imbibe.

"Methinks yer lovely sister is quite intoxicating enough for me." Sean said, then leaned closer toward Niall. "Perhaps ye would do us the honor of giving us some peace now?"

Lachlann's jaw dropped. "We would miss Tommy's cooking. I can smell it!"

Niall put an arm around his friend. "We will allow them their time, Lachlann." He spoke over his shoulder. "We will see to ourselves."

Sean pushed the door shut, having to wiggle it into place to do so. He turned toward Thomasina who went with him, their hands still joined. His chest expanded at the sight of her standing there. "Ye are lovely dressed as a lass, my Thomasina."

She held his gaze. "I like being *yer* Thomasina."

He closed the distance pulling their joined hands to his chest, untied the bow, and kissed her upturned palm.

"Was that unkind of us to kick them out into the night?" she asked.

"Not to my way of thinking." Sean moved in close, placing a kiss on her cheek. Her sweet womanly scent stirred him."Is it to yers?"

Her eyes were closed, her lips slightly parted. She shook her head. Gathering her in close, he held her tight against the length of his body. He took a deep breath, near to bursting with desire for her. That would not be the way of it. Not tonight. He needed to move slowly and see to her pleasure. Her stomach growled and they both laughed.

"Methinks ye need sustenance."

Thomasina stepped away. "Methinks ye're right. Are ye hungry?"

Only for ye. "Yea."

"It must be hot enough."

His eyes remained on her as she went to the fire. The dress swaying softly against her curves. Titillating him. "And what is this that ye make so well that it has our long-haired friend's tongue all but hanging out?"

"A mix of the hardy squash and herbs 'tis all. It stores well." She carefully removed the lid.

A delicious aroma filled the room. His own stomach gurgled. "We should eat."

"Yea." She filled two wooden plates and carried them to the trestle table where he'd dragged one of the hard benches. He motioned for her to sit beside him. "'Tis best to eat before... sleeping."

Sean suddenly cared very much about offending her with ribald comments. He knew he'd feel differently when she was attired as a lass. There had only been one woman he'd thought to impress and that was Brighit. It wasn't like that with Thomasina. He wanted her to be pleased with him as her husband, not impressed.

The food was warm and tasty. He ate with relish. "Very good."

She took a piece of the cheese and passed it to him. "I have cooked for my father and brother a very long time."

"Lovely and a good cook. What else do I not ken about ye?"

Thomasina swallowed her cheese and placed her hands on her lap. "That I feel very special to have ye as my husband."

Her declaration surprised him. A fierce need to pleasure her as his wife overtook him. No one had ever meant this much to him. He struggled to keep his breathing even, his appetite vanished, and he watched intently as she finished her food. He offered her the mead. "Just a little?"

She tipped her head and accepted it. He declined when she offered it back. He dare not allow himself to relax. He needed to be in complete control when he bedded her. Rushing her to see to his own need was not the way he wanted it to be with her. Ever.

When Sean stood beside her and extended his hand, Thomasina's heart beat faster. It was difficult to breathe. She accepted his hand and stood, fighting to appear composed despite the anxiety expanding in her gut. With a finger under her chin, he tipped her head up so he could see into her eyes.

"I want to make love to ye, Thomasina."

She swallowed then nodded, pressing her lips together before speaking. "Yea. Of course. We're husband and wife."

He smiled. A kind, warm smile that told her beyond any doubt that he understood how she was feeling.

"Apologies. I'm such a milksop."

Sean placed a finger to her lips to stop her. "Nae. Do not speak poorly of yerself. Not with me." He moved in closer, gently pulling her length against him. "I believe ye're perfect just the way ye are. Dunna be telling me otherwise."

He smelled of the outdoors. A calming scent. She took a slow breath. With her eyes closed, she imagined their bodies as they touched. His strong arms wrapping lightly around her. She snuggled in closer and they tightened in response. His solid chest beneath her cheek, the light smattering of hair she would enjoy caressing hidden beneath. His solid hips against her own, the hardened tarse against her belly, the solid legs pressing into her.

When he slipped his hand along her back, he turned her in his arms and pulled her bottom solidly against his manhood. He dipped his head to kiss the side of her head. "Ye will have pleasure as my wife."

A shiver of anticipation washed over her. It settled somewhere between her thighs. "I ken."

He turned her again and pulled back to look at her. "And I heard ye were not so worldly as all that."

She smiled, her tension easing a bit. "Yea. I talk a good talk."

When she looked up to see into his eyes, he closed the distance to her mouth. A feather light kiss stirred her passion, overwhelming her fear. She parted her lips, allowing his tongue access. His kiss became more impassioned and she matched him as he stoked the spark of desire into a flame.

His strong hands dipped again to her bottom, cupping her cheeks, pulling her up against him. "Have I told ye how much I admire yer lovely arse?"

Thomasina tried not to laugh. "Nae. Nae ye have not."

"Ye find humor in my discomfort?"

She sobered quickly. "I dunna understand."

"This fine arse," he grasped her bottom as he spoke, "filled my dreams even before I caught ye in the woods, baring yer bottom."

Thomasina gasped and started to pull away but he held her firm.

"Ye've a fine arse." He nibbled at her neck. "I dinna mean to shame ye. Never that."

"So ye did see my naked bottom?"

He groaned, pulling her in tight against him leaving no doubt what he was feeling. "Yea. It damned near killed me and seeing ye in those trews, outlining each rounded cheek."

A guttural sound emanated from deep inside him and he stilled. His breathing labored. He took a deep breath then pulled away to sit on the bench behind him, his hands on his legs.

"I lusted after ye, Thomasina. Something fierce." He licked his lips. His eyes roaming over her. As before he paused at her breasts and looked left then right.

"Tell me then how did ye ken I was a lass?"

He looked up at her and it seemed to take a moment for his answer. "I knew ye were a woman when I touched yer full breast."

Sean reached an arm toward her bosom. He traced his fingers along each breast, cupping their fullness then stroking her rigid nipples. She closed her eyes at the intensity of longing sweeping through her.

"Ye're a bonny lad." He urged her closer to stand between his legs. "A more bonny lass."

He turned his head to rest his cheek against her. She felt certain he could feel her heart beat against him.

"And 'tis fine with ye that I am not man enough?"

Thomasina reminded him of his earlier taunts.

He pulled back, a lopsided grin on his face. "Yea. 'Tis more than fine. As a lass, I find ye lacking nothing. I should not have taunted ye so but I had a hard time keeping my hands off ye."

The intensity of his gaze slowly sweeping over her heated her skin, as if it were his hands caressing her. "I want ye something fierce, Sean." She repeated his earlier words.

He looked up at her. "Yea? Ye're a brave one."

Hooking an arm behind her knees, he took her into his arms and walked to the pallet in the corner. He nuzzled through her hair, kissed her neck, then allowed her legs to drop. "Ye're a bonny one indeed," he untied the bow at the back, pulling at the laces with each word, "and methinks ye're even more bonny beneath."

The gown loosened and he slipped it down her arms. She couldn't catch her breath as he watched its movement slipping from her, revealing a shoulder. A breast. A navel. He pulled her close, his tongue circling her nipple before he sucked it into his mouth. She fought to hold back her groan of pleasure. He slid the gown down as he continued the assault of one breast and then the other. His mouth warm against her skin.

Wetness pooled in her most intimate area and she held her legs closed. She bit her lip to keep from making a sound as her body arched against him. His hand on her bottom, grasping and stroking, made her pulse quicken. She tried to keep her lips closed.

～

Sean had wondered at the responsiveness of her body at his ministrations. Cantering hips. Arching back. Grasping hands. Clearly she was aroused and that pleased him. When he saw her biting her lip, he knew why her passion seemed muted. He took a deep, shaky breath and sat down on the coffer. He was near to exploding and this wonderful, little treasure was trying not to make a sound. Perhaps he moved too fast.

"Come." Sean patted his lap. "I wish to hold my bride."

She came willingly, if a little uncertain, and sat on his lap. His eyes dropped to her rosy nipples, begging to be suckled but glanced at her face. "Kiss me, Thomasina."

He saw the flash of pleasure in her eyes. She tipped her head toward him, her lips soft against his. Timid. Then she became more forceful. Wrapping her hand around his head, she pulled him in closer as her tongue sparred with his own. He'd thought allowing her to go at her own pace might help cool his need but she was quickly pushing him over the edge.

Thomasina started to pull at his leine. "I want to see ye."

He reluctantly withdrew his hands and she stood away from him. Her lips parted, she watched as he doffed each piece of clothing. Her breathing accelerating. When he dropped his trews and his manhood sprang forth, she glanced at his face, her eyes widening. He could see the fear forming in her mind and he pulled her in close.

"Love making is not painful. 'Tis pleasurable. Perhaps the first time there may be some discomfort."

"Ye're going to rip me asunder with that thing." She sounded near to tears.

"Where is my brave, Thomasina?"

She pulled back to give him a withering look. He smiled.

"I will not rip anything but yer maidenhead which needs to be taken."

She said nothing but he could feel her body tensing.

"We can stop now if ye are afraid."

"I am not afraid." Thomasina pushed her shoulders back with the declaration.

"Then let us lie down for a bit." Sean indicated the small pallet behind them.

Thomasina slid down against the wall and turned toward him. He lay on his back. "Will ye kiss me again?"

Her face lit up. Something she did enjoy. She began with an eager kiss that made him rock hard with its unspoken promises. He stroked her side then up her thigh and again between her legs. Her body was eager if her mind was not yet ready.

He covered her and cupped her breasts. With a firm tongue he stroked her nipples into hard buds, her moans a balm to his lust inflamed body. When she reached to pull his hip closer to her, he pushed her down. "Not yet. Let me show ye pleasure, Thomasina."

Moving to her stomach, he kissed and laved as he dropped lower. He positioned himself between her legs, nibbling a hip as he worked his way to her core. He could smell her need and it nearly set him off. Her wetness was sweet on his tongue and he stroked her, long and deep. She pivoted, rocking against his mouth. He dipped a finger in and she bucked up, nearly dislodging him. She grasped at his head, pulling him in tighter. Out of necessity, he imagined himself in the cold ocean, the water gripping him. Then he tried to imagine standing naked in the cold snow. His body demanded distraction. There'd never been such a need for him to hold off his own pleasure but he would not be disappointing her.

Thomasina tried to focus on him. He watched her intently as if measuring her reaction. The pleasure he was giving her demanded all her attention. Her eyes closed and a guttural sound emanated from her throat. She reached to draw him up against her again.

He put his lips to her ear as he positioned himself between her legs. "Is túsa mo chroí." *Ye are my heart.*

He moved in a slow rhythm.

This was not something she'd ever been warned of. Coupling was not to be enjoyable but this… this was more than enjoyable.

"Shall I end sooner?" He plunged deep within, touching her womb, pressing his hips against her then stilled. The pain, a slight sting then gone.

She finally looked at him. The words came back to her of the earlier claims of wanting to be done with him. She smiled.

"Oh yea, I do prefer ye not end sooner—" She gasped at the sudden, deep thrust. "—but much later."

He grabbed her close against him, his hand cupping her bottom, nestling his nose in her hair.

"Good. I would not want to be exhibiting brutish behavior."

And he gently moved against her, fitting perfectly between her thighs despite his massive muscles. He filled her perfectly.

"Well, maybe a little brutish."

There was that noise again from deep inside. She tried to swallow it down.

"Nae, my Thomasina. Dunna hold back. Let me hear yer pleasure."

He suddenly slowed, entering her with long, deliberate thrusts.

Her groan was loud in the small space. He did know what he was about.

"Yea. That is the way. Can ye feel me inside ye?"

She rocked her hips against him, pivoting to take him even deeper. The need for something she didn't understand swept over her. She dug her nails into his back. Urging him on. Wanting more. Wanting— something.

"Easy." Sean's voice was low, vibrating through her. "Feel me in ye. We are one."

Thomasina focused on the feelings that were rushing over her. Close to some pinnacle she didn't comprehend until it burst through her. Her muscles convulsed around him. He responded with more deliberation, quickening his pace. His roar of pleasure erupted with his final thrust and he collapsed beside her, pulling her up against him.

She sighed. "Yea, Sean. Ye pleasured me well."

Sean burst into a huge grin and hugged her to him. "Yea. As ye did me."

"I dinna expect—I dinna ken what to expect."

He kissed the top of her head. "I dinna expect such pleasure myself."

She pulled back to look at him. "Truly?"

"Yea. I am not one for idle words."

"Idle words?"

"What I say is true." He looked her in the eyes. "Ye were the one

intended for me. I need ye by my side always. I'll protect ye with my life."
He pulled her in for a passionate kiss. "Mo chroí go deo thú." *My heart is
yers forever.*

CHAPTER 16

Sean awakened to banging on the door. It took him a moment to remember where he was but he knew immediately the small body tucked beside him was his wife—Thomasina. He kissed the top of her head and moved away trying not to disturb her.

It was still dark. He donned his trews and went to the door. Lachlann stood there, cupping his hands to his mouth as he tried to keep warm. "We found a boatman but we need to go now. No sign of the Normans."

Sean wanted to make love to Thomasina again in the night but she hadn't awakened. "Yea. Give us a minute."

Shutting the door, Sean returned to light the candle and bring it closer to the bed. The bloodstain beneath them was proof enough that she was indeed his. The smile on her face as she slept told him she was happy about it.

"Thomasina." He kneeled beside the pallet, a hand on her shoulder. "Mo mhíle stór, we need to go now."

She frowned, shielding her eyes from the light. "'Tis the middle of the night. We will not be able to see anything."

"'Tis almost sunrise. Lachlann says we need to go now."

She sat up still half-asleep. Her nakedness called to him and he cupped a breast as he moved in nearer. "If I had my way, I would wake ye slowly and pleasure ye until ye cried out my name."

She smiled, her eyes partly closed in her weariness. "Did I not call yer name? I knew it was ye and none other that made such sweet love to me, mo mhíle stór." She pursed her lips toward him for a kiss.

He kissed her, rubbing his lips against hers. "Good day, my sweet Thomasina."

"Yea. 'Tis that."

Thomasina stood up and stretched her delectable body. Sean had a hard time keeping himself focused on dressing with her body all but calling out to him.

"Are ye sore?"

She stilled and closed her eyes as if assessing her body from the inside. "Maybe a little here." She opened her eyes and offered a most fetching expression while pressing her hand between her legs. "'Twas a necessary pain that resulted in much more pleasure."

"Are not ye the worldly one now?" Sean pulled at the sheet, removing it from the pallet, and wrapped it up to take with them in case there was need of any proof. "Come now."

She accepted his outstretched hand. Even as they opened the door, a dull light was making its way toward the sunrise. Lachlann handed Sean the lead to Niall's riderless horse and smiled at Thomasina. "Ye made it through the night I see."

"Yea. Even with my big, strapping husband, I survived just fine."

Sean mounted and reached down to pull her up in front of him. "And I survived just fine as well."

Lachlann's face blanked before he broke into a laugh. "I had no concern for ye, man."

He jumped onto his horse. By the time they made the shore, the sun was clearing the horizon but a heavy mist hung over the water making it difficult to see. Niall came out of the trees. "The boatman will be here anon."

Sean dismounted and took a quick scan of their surroundings. He reached up to take Thomasina by her small waist and help her down. He stopped, holding her just short of touching her feet to the ground. "A kiss for my efforts?"

She smiled and kissed him. He held her against him, wrapping both arms around her when she would have pulled away. His lips demanding more, she wrapped her arms around his neck to deepen the kiss.

"Thank ye for yer efforts," she teased him.

Sean smiled back but didn't put her down. "Can ye say goodbye to yer brother? And his friend?"

She glanced behind him where her brother waited beside Lachlann. "Yea. Do ye think it be forever?"

"Nae. We will return if 'tis what ye want."

She closed her eyes and drew a deep breath before looking at him with a smile. "Thank ye for that as well."

Niall started toward the shore, the sound of the surf the only noise "I think this is the boat now."

Sean slipped his head through the rope on his shield, securing it to his back and took the sack. They followed behind.

Like a ghost in the mist, the longboat appeared with a single man. "Hail."

Sean's fist clenched. Something in the voice was familiar. He thrust Thomasina behind him and withdrew his sword. "Stay here."

Niall was almost to the shore, Lachlann beside him. Sean surged forward just as the heavily-cloaked boatman waded into the water, bent toward his boat.

"'Tis a trap," Sean said as he sped past them.

The words were shouted as the man turned toward him, cloak thrown over his shoulder revealing his mail and his sword in hand.

Sean raised his own sword, intercepting any danger to Niall or Lachlann. Engaging the boatman, blade to blade they slid down to the grip, face to face, and shoved against each other. The soldier's cloak quickly soaking, dragging him down, making his movements difficult.

In the distance, the sound of horses and shouting men could be heard as other soldiers advanced onto the beach. Sean urged the man deeper into the waves until he stumbled back, his sword tangled in the material and swamped by the surf. With the hilt of his sword, Sean gave a quick downward thrust to the man's face. The blood mixed with the water as he went under.

With high steps through the crashing waves, Sean rushed to help Niall and Lachlann. Their swords at the ready, the two faced the oncoming soldiers. Sean came up alongside them.

"This is not looking good." The intensity of emotion came through in Lachlann's voice.

No one responded. A high-pitched sound carried to Sean over the sound of the waves. His heart jumped into his throat at the sight of Thomasina running toward the beach, her hands flailing in the air. It sounded like she yelled, "Stop!"

Sean ran toward the closest mounted soldier, his arms wide, as he shouted his war cry. As expected, the horse reared up. The next two soldiers were prepared, one even jumping down to meet him on foot with a pole axe.

"Stop!" Thomasina's shrill cry carried to the soldiers. The one on foot turned toward her. Sean surged forward, shoving his pole arm into the air. His sword found its mark.

"'Tis Aldred. The little man is with him." Lachlann's voice carried to Sean but it didn't make any difference to him. He needed to get Thomasina safely away. The boat drifted closer to the shore with the incoming tide but it would be drifting out just as easily. He needed to get to it.

"My lord," a voice called out behind Sean as he yanked the soldier off his horse, landing him flat on his back.

"We have word from Lord John, Earl of Kent. He sends a treatise of protection over the Eire man."

Sean smashed his sword pommel into the Norman's face, the sound of breaking bone gratifying.

"Halt!" It was the lord who had ordered Sean's beheading.

Sean ran toward the boat just as the water threatened to suck it back into deeper water.

"Halt, Normans!"

Sean grabbed at the rope from the boat dragging it closer to shore and looked behind to find Thomasina far too close to the soldiers. Niall and

Lachlann stood a short distance from him. The Lord sat atop his horse where a small man was running toward him. He held something over his head. He seemed familiar to Sean.

"Sean," Niall called to him, his hands cupped to help his voice carry.

Sean reached Thomasina in three steps, throwing her over his shoulders.

"Niall is calling to ye." Thomasina's voice implored him to stop.

"I see to yer protection. I will not let them harm ye." He placed Thomasina inside the boat. "Stay down."

She lay on her belly, one hand holding the side of the small boat. "I think the attack has stopped."

Sean glanced again toward the little man dressed in mail. Yes. A man at the Priory. The Earl's man.

Taking a run into the waves, Sean pushed the boat away from the shore. He jumped in at the last second and grabbed an oar.

When Thomasina moved to sit up, he urged her down. "I dunna want ye to become a target."

She peered over the edge. "But they no longer fight."

Niall's call carried to him. "Sean! Lord John has sent his protection."

Lord John was Peter's close friend. And then there was the talkative soldier, Mort. Sean realized the little man was, indeed, Mort himself. Sean scanned the soldiers. All had their weapons lowered. The ones on horseback now waited behind their liege lord.

"Ye can sit up." Sean offered his hand.

"Do ye think what he said is true? Can there be word from York? Was someone sent?"

Aldred stood beside his two friends looking quite a bit travel worn. "Methinks yer brother may have seen to *my* protection this time."

When the boat drifted in on the next wave, Sean jumped out and took hold of the rope. He pulled it toward Niall, beaching it on the sand. He picked Thomasina up and out of the boat. Her feet never touching the water. Holding her hand and still positioning her behind him, he approached the three friends. The dark lord urged his horse a bit closer.

"Is there something ye neglected to tell me of?" Sean directed his question to Niall.

Niall laughed. "Yea. Aldred went off to York as soon as we heard no one had been sent."

"What say you?" The Lord's angry voice rang out, edged with defensiveness. "I dispatched a man to York." He glanced at the soldiers on either aside. They avoided his eyes. "Did I not?"

"We have not heard back," the soldier to his right answered. "Regardless, he still murdered the only witness to the killings."

The man called Mort stepped past him to take Sean's hand. "Lord John sends his greetings along with his protection and that of the King, Sean of Drogheda." He turned back to the soldier who had spoken. "If the man you speak of was Ivan, I can assure you, all that he told you was a lie. If he has been killed by this man's hand," Mort indicated Sean, "it was a job well-done and long overdue."

Mort reached up to place his arm on Sean's shoulder. "Peter sends his regards as well and wishes you safe travels home."

Peter, Brighit's new husband. "How fares Brighit?"

Mort nodded, a slow nod as if he had knowledge beyond what was said. "She and Peter are happy. They wish the same for you, Sean."

Brighit's last words to Sean filled his mind.

There is a wonderful woman out there intended for you alone. Open your heart so that love may find you.

"My thanks, Mort." He brought Thomasina to the forefront. "I would make known to ye, Thomasina. My wife."

Mort tipped his head to Sean then bowed with great comportment. "A pleasure, dear lady."

Sean's chest could expand no further. His joy complete. "And please tell Brighit she was correct."

Mort paused then nodded. "I will pass on your message."

The lord dropped from his horse to approach Sean. "I fear in my grief I have listened to the wrong man. I will pray for more wisdom in my dealings forthwith. Forgive me."

Sean tipped his head. "Ivan meant to cause problems here. Killing as many Normans as he could was only the beginning of his plans."

Niall wrapped an arm around his sister's shoulder. "So do ye still have to leave now?"

Sean understood his sadness. Where he had sadness, Sean had happiness. He offered a gracious smile. "Niall, I am long overdue back to my clan. The tide is right. Now is the time we must leave."

"But ye've no one to man the boat." Lachlann pointed toward the empty vessel.

Sean tipped his head. "Ah, my friend. I never said I was unable to man the boat myself. Thomasina will be in good hands."

Niall gathered her close. "Be well, sister."

She nodded and kissed his cheek before withdrawing.

The moisture on her cheeks could not be attributed to the surf alone. Sean moved in close. "Will it be well with ye, mo mhíle stór?"

Her eyes rounded. She swallowed hard as if trying to force down all the sadness threatening to overwhelm her. "I ken ye are my tomorrow. I feel a little sad saying goodbye to yesterday 'tis all."

He tipped her chin up. "I will make ye forget yer yesterdays." He kissed her. "And these men will indeed be part of yer tomorrow. That I promise ye."

Her expression lightened with his words and he helped her into the boat. Settling behind her, Sean raised his knees to protect her on both sides. He took the oar. "I just wish I had been able to get Tadhg's damn knife. I will never hear the end of it."

"Oh, wait! Niall!" She jumped up without warning, nearly overturning the small vessel. She held her hand out, palm up. "Niall! The knife!"

Niall frowned as if thinking then nodded, a huge smile across his face. He dug into the bag at his waist. "Here ye go, brother! Ye can thank me when next we meet."

He tossed it to Sean who caught it.

"Yer friend's knife! Yea?" Thomasina asked.

Sean opened the blades of the intricately carved knife. "Yea. The very same."

"Niall found it on the floor at the blacksmith's."

"Glad I am that he did."

She settled down in front of him. The ocean's current pulled them further out to sea.

"At least I will not have to hear about *that* from Tadhg." He bent his head in a scolding frown when her eyes came back to him. "Ye—on the other hand. I will never hear the end of marrying ye!" He pulled her in close. "The knife I could gladly have gone on without and withstood his anger. But ye? I could never withstand a life without ye." He placed a gentle kiss on her lips. "And I would have it no other way."

"Nor would I."

THE END

ABOUT THE AUTHOR

Aside from two years spent in the wilds of the Colorado mountains, Ashley York is a proud life-long New Englander and a hardcore romantic. She has an MA in History which brings with it a love for primary documents and the smell of musty old libraries. With her author's imagination, she likes to write about people who could have lived alongside those well-known giants from the past.

Connect with her online at
Website: www.ashleyyorkauthor.com